MONEY MAN

Sandra M. Bush

SANDRA M. BUSH

Year of the Book
135 Glen Avenue
Glen Rock, PA 17327

ISBN 13: 978-1-945670-71-8
ISBN 10: 1-945670-71-1

Library of Congress Control Number: 2017963572

DEDICATION

For Todd

ACKNOWLEDGMENTS

With thanks and appreciation...

To my husband, Todd: My love, my inspiration and the bright light that guides me through every dark tunnel.

To my daughters, Chelsea and Monica: For your love, encouragement and technical support over the years.

To Charlie Bieber, Wade Fulton and Cindy Hospador: Thank you for being my earliest readers and for offering support and gentle editorial suggestions—even when I didn't listen.

To my friend and coach, Demi Stevens: Thank you for helping me weave the threads to connect my story and for pushing me to have the courage to complete this project.

And posthumously to my parents, Albert and Mabel Acri: For giving me a lifetime of unconditional love, and for being my first and biggest fans.

PROLOGUE

Tom Frye is rich. And he likes making other people rich. Or at least he used to. But that was before.

CHAPTER ONE

Tom winced when his bipolar secretary's name popped up on the caller ID of the car's digital dashboard.

"Peggy, what's up?" he asked.

"Mina Stab is worried that you'll run over one of her cats. She wants you to park outside the main gate and walk up to the house."

"Are you kidding me? It's like the length of two football fields," Tom roared. "Freaking cats. Does she realize I'm wearing a suit, for God's sake?"

"I don't think Mina cares what you're wearing. She's worried about her cats. Oh, can you hold on? Derrick's trying to call me."

Tom slammed his hand against the steering wheel. *Peggy. Why does she always put me on hold?* And Mina's damn cats. Tom's family owned two—both female—and his wife and daughters adored them.

Yeah, but I'm always the one to discover their hairballs in my stocking feet.

He wasn't an animal lover, but he had come by it honestly. His parents had been too busy traveling. His only pet had been a hamster, Boz, tragically sucked up in the vacuum cleaner by his mother while she cleaned the cage. That ended that.

He banged on the steering wheel again, anxious to reconnect. Today for a change, Peggy didn't keep him waiting long.

"I'm back. Sorry," Peggy said, not sounding the least bit apologetic. "What were you going to say?"

"It's ninety degrees outside," Tom said. "Mina is insane. Why do I keep her as a client?"

"Because she's filthy rich," Peggy said. "She knows you're afraid of her."

"I am not afraid of Mina Stab." Tom clenched and unclenched his left fist. "If she thinks she can find a better financial advisor, let her try," he said. "Who else would put up with the ridiculous shit she puts me through? In fact—"

"Look," Peggy interrupted, "more sympathetic I could not be, but Derrick is on the other line again. I gotta go. Watch out for those cats."

He heard the line go dead.

Peggy showed up late for work a lot, and the excuses always involved her husband. Derrick needed her help to pick out an outfit, or make his lunch. All day long, their co-dependency kept them tethered to their cell phones. And on company time, too. Repulsive.

Fuck you, Peggy. You just talked to him thirty seconds ago.

Tom pounded the steering wheel a third time and kept driving. He wished he could fire her, but he didn't have the energy to look for a better assistant right now.

Forty-five minutes later, he turned down the lane to the Stab estate. He parked and found himself facing a pair of large stone lions perched atop marble blocks that guarded the gateway to their farm. With jaws wide open, they appeared ready to roar and spring into life at any moment.

Before he got out of the Mercedes, he glanced in the rearview mirror and admired his reflection. He smiled and paused to adjust a stray lock of brown hair and straightened his tie. He grabbed what he needed from the car, locked it and walked toward the gate.

Tom pressed the intercom button at the security gate and heard an obnoxious buzz. He waited for her to answer.

"Yes?" Mina's mocking voice blared through the speaker.

"Mina, it's Tom. I understand you want me to walk all the way up to the house?" *Bitch.*

"Well, thank God for small favors," Mina said. "Don't tarry. You're already late."

The buzzer blasted and the gate swung open. Tom rolled his eyes toward the surveillance camera.

As he sprinted to the Stab's farmhouse, the country air tickled his nose and made him sneeze. Large land mines of dung clotted in clumps of mud and red clay where grass used to grow. The pungent smell masked those of the honeysuckle and roses growing along the split rail fence.

While he walked, he spotted a rusty old plow, two weathered sawhorses and antique tools scattered everywhere. Despite the clutter, the landscaping was spectacular. The Stab's gardeners had planted dozens of rose bushes, native plants and endless rows of annual and perennial flowers.

So this is where their money is going.

Tom saw the Stab's house ahead in the distance—a modest brick colonial with faded aluminum siding and a pathetic weather vane leaning to one side.

In contrast stood the stately red barn built last year. The massive building sat off to the far right and dwarfed the house by comparison. Cows mooed in the distance, and several horses grazed nearby. As if on cue, they stopped eating and stared as he approached. He kept walking and swatted at something buzzing in his ear.

Uh oh. Is that a fly or a bee?

Tom walked toward the Stab's back porch, maneuvering around animal pens and overgrown garden plots.

Why in the hell don't they ever use their damn front porch?

Tom slogged ahead, dodging ditches, large rocks, potholes and animal dung on the unpaved path. Discarded gardening tools, bags of fertilizer and empty coffee cans were everywhere. He tried not to step in anything gross, but no luck.

Immersed in shit. Yep, this is my life.

"Damn it! My shoes." His new Italian loafers. Ruined. He had owned them less than a week.

Loud buzzing distracted him. He whipped around and saw the culprit. *Wasps. Where are they coming from? It looks like a half a dozen, at least. Are you supposed to swat at them or ignore them?*

As he got closer to the house, a galloping horse made its way toward him. It snorted, pranced and tossed its mane, then advanced, trumpeting a loud whinny, and stared at Tom. Flies swarmed around its head and tail. They buzzed and whirred. As Tom stared back into the animal's large brown eyes, a quiver of fear rumbled in the pit of his stomach.

It's like that horse knows I'm afraid. Jesus, I'm a six-foot, 225-pound wimp.

Still, the horse moved nearer, its scent heavy with hay and manure. The smell nauseated Tom. Only a split rail fence divided man and beast. Almost on cue, the horse took two quick steps closer and snorted loudly. The horse's breath breezed over the top of his head. He stepped back and away from the animal. Apparently bored with the game, the horse then galloped off toward the barn.

Thank God.

The buzzing insects distracted Tom again. *Are they following me? Jesus. Covered in mud, stalked by a crazed horse, and now trying not to get stung. What a great job I have.*

He forged on and tried to avoid walking in the dirt. But yesterday's rain had created a thick, slimy mud. It covered the sidewalk, and clung to the cuff of Tom's pants and his ruined shoes. He walked on the crumbling, cracked sidewalk to the back of the house and mopped his sweaty face and neck with his pocket square. The cloud of wasps buzzed all around him but he resisted the urge to swat at them.

Yellow Jacket escorts. Perfect.

The closer he got to the house, the louder the buzz. Then he saw the enormous wasp nest hanging near the corner of the porch, nestled next to one of the rainspouts. To make matters worse, out of nowhere, a large mastiff bounded over barking and growling. The dog charged at Tom, its coat caked with mud, drool flying from its jaws. Tom managed to keep his composure and climb the steps. The dog continued to bark but kept its distance.

Amidst the commotion, Tom saw Mina peering out behind filmy curtains. He knocked on the door, but she took her time, making him wait a good minute or so before she opened it. The dog continued to bark and growl, and the wasps zoomed in next to his head.

Finally Mina opened the door, dressed in an animal print shirt, a pair of tight, black capri pants and high spike-heeled sandals. Tom realized she looked just like the woman on his wife's Chico's catalog at home. Her perfect blonde bobbed hair and heavy, artful makeup masked her age well.

Mina snorted and surveyed Tom's appearance. "Honestly, Thomas, can't you dress professionally when you visit your clients? What can I expect you're doing with my stock portfolio? You look as if you've been mucking out the stables."

"Well, Mina, if I'd known I'd be walking in from the gate, I'd have brought my hiking boots."

"Indeed. I assumed after all this time you would remember my concerns. I never dreamed you would come without appropriate footwear!"

Mina slapped her hands together, as if ridding them of imaginary dirt. She pointed to Tom's feet.

"Off with your shoes—in fact, take off all your clothes. I'll have Mason bring you something to change into."

"Excuse me? Take off my what?"

"I said strip. Here on the porch should be fine. I'll have Mason hose off your things when he brings you something else to wear."

"Thanks, but I'll take care of my clothes when I get back to the office. Aren't you worried about that nest? Over there in the corner? Those wasps followed me most of the way here."

"Wasps? Thomas, are you familiar with the critical shortage of pollinators in the world now? It's an international crisis. Honestly!"

She stormed back into the house and threw him a dirty look as she slammed the door. No doubt the hive served as both ornamental and functional for the Stabs.

Tom waited on the porch as the mammoth dog howled and wasps played ring around the rosy above his head. Mason the butler eventually showed up with fresh "clothes," looking like a hipster metrosexual. He wore a black shirt and pants, with silver clogs on his feet. He had silver hoops hanging from his earlobes and a stickpin stud in his left eyebrow. His black, highlighted hair sported sprigs of green and red tufts.

Bile rose up in Tom's throat. Everything around him smelled like shit. *Probably from every farm animal known to man. The Stabs too. And what about that damn wasp's nest? Thank God, I'm not allergic. At least I don't think so.*

Tom forced the thoughts out of his head. Out of the corner of his eye, he saw Mina return to the porch.

"Strip, Thomas!" She clapped her hands like a child.

Dr. Stab appeared at his wife's side, looking ready for an afternoon of tennis in a flashy purple Lacoste shirt, and roomy white Bermuda shorts that concealed his sizable stomach. On his feet he wore New Balance sneakers and white socks decorated with tiny purple crowns around the cuff.

Three Siamese cats circled between their owners' feet. Two rubbed up against Dr. Stab's leg, arching their backs and lifting their tails in greeting. Mina reached down and lifted the smallest of the three into her arms. She rubbed her face against the tiny cat's head.

When Mason handed Tom a pair of dark blue operating room scrubs, the Stabs shared a laugh at his expense.

Unbelievable! Forcing him to change clothes.

He moved as far out of sight as possible, next to a stack of old paint cans on the side of the porch. His cheeks flamed with humiliation as he stripped off his clothes.

"Those bastards!" he said under his breath. "I'll get them for this."

Tom reluctantly put his clothing in the black garbage bag Mina threw at him. He resigned himself to go inside and get this over with.

I'm not taking their bullshit abuse today. I need to keep my sense of humor.

He took a deep breath, and steadied himself. A well-manicured paw stopped him in his tracks.

"Hold it right there," Mina said. "You forgot about your socks. Here, you can put these on. I have no desire to see your bare feet."

She threw Tom a pair of flimsy, blue disposable booties. Like those shoe coverings used by plumbers and electricians.

"Either take those socks off and put the booties on, or come back another time when you're better prepared," Mina said when Tom hesitated. He then peeled off his socks, tossed them in the bag and put on the booties.

After a final inspection, Mina sniffed her approval and waved Tom into the house. The interior looked tidier than he remembered from the last visit. *Mason's job description must include cleaning the house as well as hosing off messy visitors.*

Stacks of fashion magazines and animal reference books covered the dining room table. Catnip mice and dog chew toys scattered the hallway floor. A partially eaten dog bone had been abandoned next to the doormat. Tom surmised the dog preferred snacking on guests instead.

Mason steered him to the kitchen table, where Dr. Stab sat sipping coffee next to a tray of bagels, a quart of half-and-half, a container of Stevia, and a fifth of Bankers Club.

Dr. Stab limply shook Tom's hand, not bothering to stand. He quickly rubbed that hand on his trousers, as if he'd touched something sticky. Mason lurked in the doorway, until Dr. Stab and Mina waved him off.

Ha. No free financial advice for the butler this morning, I guess.

Tom struggled to maintain his composure. He sat at the table, spread out his documents on the sticky wooden surface and launched into his review of the Stab's stock portfolio. He reminded them that under his management, their account was up seven percent since the previous year. The bonds, mutual funds and IRAs he'd chosen for them were all doing well. He tried to sound enthusiastic because, after all, their account had done well. Deep down though, he knew it would never be good enough.

"Well now, listen here, Tom," Dr. Stab said. "I realize this performance is adequate. But you know, I'm not that impressed. In fact, after talking to my peers at Hopkins, I'm disappointed. I hear they all have skyrocketing gains in their accounts. One chap I spoke with said he was up fourteen percent. Imagine that. Why that's double what ours is doing. What kind of explanation do you have for that? Why aren't we seeing returns like his? I pay you a lot of money to manage these accounts. I expect more from you."

Dr. Harry Stab, a renowned plastic surgeon, operated mostly in the Baltimore and D.C. suburbs. A pompous, overconfident jackass, Stab enjoyed working on the high society types. He was handsome in a puffy, paunchy, mature way—too tanned, a tiny bit gray, and far too smug.

In the upper crust social circles, if you'd had some "work" done, Dr. Stab was the surgeon responsible. He flaunted his skills with silicone and saline, promising to create perkiness and volume out of sheer vanity and thin air.

Dr. Stab oozed impropriety and bragged about his patient list every time he saw Tom. Just last quarter, he had shared news of a freshening up for one of the local anchors on the Channel 3 News Team, Kim L'Orange.

When they'd met for lunch, Stab boasted all the hot nurses at the hospital came to him for their breast augmentations. He suggested he was intimate with these women, but Tom figured he didn't have the balls to ever cheat on Mina. Tom thought at the very most, maybe he pawed women when they were under anesthesia.

Tom envisioned Stab lingering over bared bosoms in the consultation room, using washable markers and sketches to illustrate the perfect pair. He pictured the surgeon's deft hands lifting and separating the breasts of young mothers, promising to restore them to pre-pregnancy buoyancy.

Stab kept blathering, but Tom snapped back to reality and interrupted. "Harry, come on. Be fair. I can't speculate on what kind of account your friend has. His broker may have him in some extremely aggressive products. Something that you, by the way, have told me you weren't interested in. For your portfolios, we chose a moderately aggressive mix of stocks that would lend to steady growth over time. After all, you can't expect me to treat your retirement accounts like I'm a day trader or something."

Stab made a snorting sound and took another sip from his cup.

"There's no predicting some of this," Tom said. "You've gotta be patient. Your account is up significantly compared to the market gains. The account's performance speaks for itself."

Tom blew out a big breath and closed his eyes to regroup. When he opened his eyes, both of the Stabs were staring at him. Mina looked amused.

A retired nurse, she had maintained her Swedish passport and scoffed at the idea of dual citizenship. Icy, blonde, svelte, and immaculately dressed, at fifty-plus Mina still looked stunning. She wore stylish, trendy outfits designed for much younger women, but pulled it off. Her rock solid physique enabled the charade. Only the skin directly beneath her chin and the upper part of her neck betrayed her with its fragile, crepe-like appearance.

Yet, despite her well-preserved beauty, Mina Stab thrived on emasculating men. With a mere frosty glance, most felt their balls shrivel in retreat. Tom girded his loins and braced himself.

Mina cleared her throat, "Well, thank you for clarifying that, Thomas. I'm sure you know what you're talking about. But what I want to ask you is something that's been on my mind for quite some time." She paused and looked at Tom for acknowledgment. He nodded in perplexed agreement.

Saved by Mina? Interesting.

"Yes, well, you know how proud I am of my Swedish ancestry. I'd like to invest in something that reflects my heritage. Something I can be proud of and can share with my children someday. I want to pass along shares of a significant Swedish stock. What do you think?" Mina smiled and waited for Tom's answer.

"Well, that's an interesting idea. Off the top of my head, I can think of a couple car companies. Or I can check with our research analysts to see if they have any recommendations." Tom smiled, thinking maybe he was in the clear.

"No, no, no," Mina said. "I already know what stock I want. I'm simply wild about the product. I buy it all the time for my family, my friends, and my business contacts. I love it so much that I can't wait to own a piece of the company."

Meanwhile, Dr. Stab continued to slurp his coffee, looking bored and flipping through the bright colored pages of his stock portfolio.

"Okay, Mina," Tom said. "What's the company?"

"I'll show you myself." She walked over to her kitchen cabinets and rummaged around. Tom heard rattling and crackling sounds, but with his back turned he couldn't see what Mina was up to.

She came back to the table wearing a broad smile. "Okay, close your eyes and hold out your hand."

Tom pretended to close his eyes and stuck out his hand. Mina put something smooth and rubbery into his palm, and closed it with a squeeze.

"Okay, you can look now. Open your hand."

When Tom opened his hand a small, red, translucent object winked in his palm: a tiny red fish.

He stared at Mina and raised an eyebrow.

"Uhh... what is this?"

Mina reached behind her back and voilà, she produced a red, blue, and yellow package decorated with a cartoonish red fish. The fish smiled back at him.

"Silly Thomas. It's a Swedish Fish. I want to buy stock in the company that makes this wonderful candy."

Tom stared at the gelatinous fish in his hand, all smooth and now slightly sticky because his palms had started to sweat. "Ah, oh, okay. Hmmm," he said, and popped it into his mouth.

"Don't tell me you've never had them? They're marvelous. A product for all ages! Sweet, chewy, satisfying. I adore them."

"Huh, well, Mina, I, ah, I really don't know what to say!" *Jesus, the stupidity of this woman.*

Mina smiled and chomped on the candy. She handed over the open bag, encouraging Tom to share in the confection.

"Go on, silly. They are delicious. You must try them. Go ahead!"

Well, for the love of God, force-fed now.

Tom complied and sampled the goods.

Okay, they are tasty, but I'd rather save my extra calories for beer. What the hell, when in Rome...

He munched along with the Stabs, until he heard a terrible crack in his jaw.

What do I do? I can't spit it out. Mina is still going on and on about how wonderful it would be to own this stock.

He kept smiling and nodding, but now he was desperate. He could feel the rogue piece of broken filling in his mouth. Ever so carefully, he pushed the sticky wad of candy, tooth, and filling to one side of his cheek. *Maybe I can store it away, like a chipmunk, until I can get out of here.*

He couldn't break one of his most sacred, most cardinal rules—no matter what the circumstances. He never used the client's bathroom. Ever.

"Mina, this is delicious, but I don't know if it's a publicly traded company." His words slurred. He tried to swallow some of the gooey saliva filling his mouth. "I'll check into it," he mumbled, but speaking was difficult.

He tried to swallow again. "Did you want anything else? I need to get back to the office. Got another appointment. Can we follow up after I check this out?" Tom tried to smile, although by now his mouth throbbed. He concentrated on not swallowing the blob.

"Well, check into it, Tom," Dr. Stab said, "because Mina has her heart set on it. Let us know what you find out. If it's not possible, start looking for another Swedish product for us to add to our portfolio. I'll double check the quarterly summary you dropped off."

Stab practically pushed him out the door.

"Goodbye. We'll talk later," Tom said and tilted his head back slightly. He fought the overwhelming urge to spit.

"Good day, Thomas," Mina said. She paused at the end table near the door, grabbed a tissue from the box, and threw it at him. "Oh, and Thomas? You're drooling. It's most unattractive."

CHAPTER TWO

Tom's bizarre appointment with the Stabs left him exhausted and anxious. Luckily the deserted back road offered him the opportunity to change clothes in the car before he got back on the road. The car's navigation system normally estimated the trip back to Cray at an hour and a half. Today, with construction and traffic, it took three.

The satellite radio blared classic rock and Tom pounded his steering wheel to the beat. Over and over he played the day's events in his head, wishing he could erase it from his brain.

What kind of sick fucks force someone to strip before going into their house? Ugh, it makes me want to punch something.

His hand twitched, aching to chuck his water bottle at the "stop/slow" flagmen ahead. *No rush to keep traffic moving. Just chain-smoke and talk on your walkie-talkies.*

To distract himself, Tom called his dentist, Dr. Kirby, but the office had closed for lunch. By the time they returned his call an hour later, he had only moved a few miles closer, and his head was exploding with a splitting migraine. "The soonest we can get you in is ten days from today," the receptionist said.

Ten days, my ass. Guess I'm looking for a new dentist now, too.

He wanted to get home, kick off his shoes, put his feet up, and zone out watching FOX News. Or a football game. Tom finally pulled the Mercedes into their four-car garage, turned off the vehicle and rubbed his throbbing temples. He grabbed his briefcase and tossed the dirty scrubs into the trash, which had become mud-covered on the long trek back from Mina's porch.

Inside the house, instead of looking through the pile of mail stacked on the kitchen counter, he grabbed a bottle of beer from the fridge. An icy cold Heineken sounded perfect, but after the long drive, he needed to hit the head first.

Afterward, he set the bottle on the vanity and frowned at his reflection in the bathroom mirror.

Jesus, I look terrible.

He opened his mouth wide to get a better look at the tooth. It throbbed now, just like his head, and agitated the side of his tongue where it rubbed against it.

The kitchen, his favorite room, was the central hub of activity for the Frye Family. Sea-foam green walls and high white ceilings showcased its light maple cabinets. Black speckled granite countertops accented the oak floors—the kitchen Vicky had always wanted.

Perched at the center island on leather barstools sat his two daughters. Eighteen-year-old Jane, the eldest, was a rebellious, redheaded academic powerhouse. Long ago, she'd earned a reputation in the family as being good at everything, and nice to no one. She played tennis, the piano and planned to graduate number two in her class. Fierce. Competitive. Beautiful.

Sixteen-year-old Sophie was blonde, bubbly and charming with eyes the color of the Mediterranean. Sweet but sly, she charmed her father into whatever she wanted. She had a slew of male admirers, and more friends than anybody could keep track of.

Tom joked how lucky he was to live with three beautiful women—a blonde, a brunette and a redhead. *Thank Christ they're not ugly. So many men have ugly wives and children.*

"Hi honey, how was your day?" Vicky rose from her seat at the kitchen table to give him a hug, but wrinkled her nose in disapproval when he pulled off his jacket and flung it over a chair. "Yuck. What's all over your pants?"

"Fine. Great. Couldn't have been better," he said. "Drove to fucking Maryland to see *Dr. Plastics* and his wife. Oh, plus I lost part of a filling and can't get in to see the dentist for over a week." He gravitated to the stack of letters and shuffled through the bills and junk mail.

"Watch your language around the girls," Vicky said, her dark eyes flashing. "How on earth did you break your tooth?"

"Have you listened to any of their conversations lately? Oh, hello girls." He reached over and patted each daughter on the head. Jane swatted his hand away. "Anyway, my tooth? Long story. The Stabs want to invest in a Swedish company so they force-fed me Swedish Fish. I don't even know if it's a publicly traded company, let alone if it's actually made in Sweden. Too bad she isn't interested in Volvo or Saab. Maybe I could've test driven a car instead of breaking a tooth." He paused and rubbed his temples.

"Right now I just want a drink and a couple of Advil. What's new here?" He continued to rifle through the mail. Most he tossed in the trash without a second glance.

"Nothing much—just the usual stuff," Vicky said. "Fix you a drink?"

"Okay, sure." Then he remembered he'd already opened a beer. He retrieved it from the bathroom sink and chugged it while rummaging through the medicine cabinet for the bottle of Advil. When he found it, he popped a handful and swallowed them with the last sip of Heineken.

Back in the kitchen, he grabbed a second beer and began pacing. It disappeared in sixty seconds flat, his old frat boy skills well honed. He tossed the empty into the recycling bin and it landed with a clink. The third one he savored a bit more, enjoying the cold, bitter brew as it hit his throat.

Tom looked over at his daughters typing away on their cells. All the estrogen-related drama left him exhausted. Even the two cats were female, and bitchy as hell. He daydreamed about running away to join the Merchant Marines, or one of those fantasy football training camp vacations.

Then, the anxiety swept over him.

What really happened today? Am I losing control? Why did I let the Stabs manipulate me? I should be happy to be home. But with two teenaged girls, and a pre-menopausal wife, I can't handle any more drama tonight.

He'd almost finished the beer when Vicky approached with his double martini. He accepted the drink and downed it in a few gulps.

His brain moved toward bliss. Numbed. But the spell was broken when Vicky glared at him from the doorway, hand on hip. "Self-medicating again, darling?" she scowled. "That's a lot of booze in five minutes or less."

Tom opened his mouth to retort, but closed it when he realized it was futile.

"Do me a favor? Go sit down and take it easy till I get back from the store. Can you eat something? So you aren't passed out by the time I get home? Something soft?"

She grabbed her purse and keys and smiled, but her eyes narrowed as she patted his cheek on her way out the door.

Tom smirked when he heard the garage door open, and Vicky's Subaru drive away. He hated the Subaru. Too practical. Too ordinary. Too boring.

His stomach growled and his mouth hurt. Between the booze and the Advil, the pain had become tolerable, but he knew he shouldn't drink this much.

Nobody understands me. Nobody appreciates me.

He trudged over to the fridge to find something that wouldn't hurt to chew. *Hmmm, yogurt? No. Apple? Definitely no. Leftover pasta? Tasty, but that would ruin my dinner. What is for dinner, anyway? Did Vicky tell me?*

He searched, desperate for something. And then he saw it. Something delicious. Something soft. Something orange. The can of Cheez Whiz! The kind with the little nozzle. Just shake the can, press the nozzle onto a cracker and bam!

But I can't eat crackers. Eh, I only want the cheese anyway. He took off the cap, opened his mouth, and sprayed the cheesy fluff right into his mouth. Then he sensed someone watching him. When he looked up, his two daughters and one of the cats, Mrs. Baby, all stared.

"Hi," he said, with a mouth full of orange processed cheese food product. "What? What do you want?"

"Dad," Jane said, "that is just too gross for words."

"Yeah, gross," Sophie echoed. "Gross, Dad."

"Mind your own business," he said, grabbing his cheese can and bottle of beer. Nestled back in his recliner, the footrest flew up, and FOX News blared from the TV.

The girls followed him into the family room and sat opposite their father, watching in silence as the buxom news anchor fired questions at her panel about whether Secretary Clinton would produce email accounts from her term as Secretary of State.

"Dad, can we watch something else?" Sophie begged. She plucked at a fluffy plaid pillow on the sofa. "We don't like news."

"Whaddya mean you 'don't like news'?" Tom said. "What do *you* want to watch? That stupid 'America's Next Top Model' or 'A Haunting'?"

"Yes, please," Sophie said.

"Anything but this," Jane added, ripping open a bag of her favorite snack, Pirate Booty.

"Go watch TV upstairs if you don't like it." Behind him he heard a rustling, followed by a scratchy, muffled sound. "Listen, girls, please don't pester me. I had a terrible day."

Jane and Sophie smiled at first, and then smirked, but Tom concentrated on the television and ignored them. The façade continued until the pair exploded in giggles.

"What? What is your problem? Why are you laughing?"

Both girls burst out laughing, and Tom realized why. Mrs. Baby, the cat, had perched above him on the recliner, licking Cheez Whiz off his shoulder.

He groaned and flung the cat off the top of the chair with the back of his hand. "Stupid cat! This animal is un-trainable," he said, jumping up to wipe the cheese off his shirt, but instead tripped over his wingtips and landed on his side.

To his credit, he held onto the can of Cheez Whiz. When he stood, he squirted a gigantic dollop into his mouth. Mrs. Baby, still quick to land on her feet after all these years, continued licking Cheez Whiz off her delicate paws and ignored everyone.

"Daddy! Be careful. She's old. Don't hurt Mrs. Baby."

"What is the lifespan for these things anyway? It seems like the cats should've died by now."

"Dad. Stop it," Jane said. "Stop torturing us."

The girls went upstairs, but not before Tom heard Sophie mutter, "Jeez, he's cranky," followed by Jane's pronouncement, "Yeah, old people are so weird."

***

When Vicky returned a short time later she found the downstairs empty, except for Mrs. Baby. She hollered hello, but heard no response.

Upstairs, she found Jane lounging on her bed, eating Pirate Booty with a chemistry book open in front of her, "Dance Moms" blaring on the TV.

Sophie, wearing only a towel, sat in front of her vanity mirror, simultaneously tweezing her eyebrows and firing off texts to one of her frenemies.

Vicky stood in the hallway and asked, "Girls, where's Daddy?"

"Who's Daddy?" Jane said. "Oh, the father figure? He's passed out on your bed, I think. He was eating Cheez Whiz straight out of the can again. He is so weird."

"Funny," Vicky said, "but he says the same thing about you, smartass." Vicky turned her attention to her younger daughter. "And for God's sake, Sophie, put on some clothes. You're dripping water all over the place."

Sophie responded with an eye roll and closed the door in her mother's face.

Vicky walked down the hall to the master bedroom to find Tom standing inside the doorway, still clutching the Cheez Whiz.

"Do you see how they treat me?" he said. "They don't respect us. Not at all, Vicky."

"If you heard me calling, and saw me talking to them, why didn't you say something?"

"I was lying down. But I got up when I heard you calling for me."

"You're drunk," she said. "Not a good example, Tom. No wonder they don't respect you."

"That's not fair," he said. "You know I had an awful day."

Vicky paused for a moment, shrugged her shoulders and turned to walk away. She turned back and called over her shoulder. "You're right," she said. "Maybe you should go lay down again. I'll bring you up some soup later."

"Okay, thanks," he said crawling back into bed with the Cheez Whiz. "Sounds good."

***

Tom started to put on his pajamas when he heard laughter downstairs. He went to the top of the steps and listened. *Ah, Vicky's on the phone.* After a few minutes he decided she was either talking to her mother, or maybe her best friend, Beth.

He heard her clicking heels walk to the fridge and then the sound of liquid pouring into a glass. Wine probably. Then more laughter. "Well, Beth, you'll never guess what he did now."

With slumped shoulders he removed a small pharmacy bottle from the nightstand drawer and dry swallowed two tablets. *Well, if one is good, two is better, right?* He crawled under the covers, curled into a fetal position and prayed for sleep.

His heart sank in his chest. Her laughter hurt more than his tooth.

CHAPTER THREE

The next morning, Tom drove south on I-83 to visit two of his most eccentric clients, the Festers. Known in the office as Tom's very own 'Beverly Hillbillies,' they received a multi-million-dollar settlement for a freak accident Dick Fester suffered working for the Mayhem Motorcycle Company.

An assembly line worker for 22 years, Fester had been at the wrong place at the wrong time. En route from his morning break, a careless forklift driver careened around a corner and hit him head on. He was thrown into a trash compacting machine, and suffered multiple injuries—including the loss of his leg just below the knee.

Fifteen years ago, a very good attorney and Tom's old frat buddy, Jim Doyle, got Fester a tidy settlement. Tom's connection with Doyle ran deep. They sometimes held financial planning seminars together, and referred clients back and forth. Mutual respect and camaraderie fueled their friendship and kept their bankrolls flush. Plenty of unfortunate accident victims needed legal and financial guidance. Even after Doyle's take, Dick Fester had a net worth of several million dollars— wealthy enough to qualify as a client for Tom.

It surprised Tom the Festers had filed a lawsuit. After all, accidents happened. Period. And although he didn't begrudge them compensation for their suffering, lawsuits spooked him. A lot of people fantasized about suing someone. The courts overflowed with sue-happy people out to make a quick buck.

Lawsuits terrified Tom; he was always afraid some radical, displeased client might sue him. It ranked among his darkest fears—and something he had no sense of humor about. His wife, Vicky, on the other hand, had a different view.

Years ago, when Vicky and Tom were still newlyweds, she was burned by a protruding tailpipe. The car had its exhaust system replaced, and the tailpipe on the tiny silver Subaru jutted at an awkward angle. When Vicky lifted the hatch to retrieve her groceries, it left her with second-degree burns and an ugly, cigar-shaped scar on her calf. Everyone at her office told her she should sue the garage, but Tom disagreed. He thought it was enough to have the garage pay her doctor bill and fix the too-long tailpipe.

"Tom, why can't we sue them?" Vicky had whined. "This scar isn't going away. Ever. I'll be embarrassed to wear shorts for the rest of my life."

"Vicky, we've been over this before. It's bad karma. Accidents happen."

Tom seldom thought about the tailpipe accident. Erased from his mind because it hadn't happened to him.

As he rounded a sharp bend in the road, the traffic had slowed to a crawl. Three or four cars in front of him chugged slowly, stuck behind a combine inching along at a snail's pace. With that many cars ahead, he knew he wouldn't be able to safely pass the farm vehicle.

"Damn it," he said. "Don't those things have to stay off state roads?" Agitated, he punched in his secretary's number on speed-dial number three.

The phone rang several times before Peggy picked up. "Good morning, Mr. Frye's office."

"Peggy," Tom shouted into the phone on his car's dashboard. "I've got a problem."

"Now what?"

Unsympathetic. As usual.

"I'm going to be late to the Festers' appointment. I'm stuck behind a combine and a couple of cars in a no passing zone."

"That's what you're in a snit about?" Peggy asked. "Why don't you just call them and tell them you're gonna be late?"

"No, Peggy. That's *your* problem," Tom screamed. "You're my secretary. You call and tell them I'm running late. It's bad enough I'll be stuck there until after lunchtime... breathing second-hand Pall Mall smoke while they slurp up their tomato juice and beer. *You call.* Understand?"

"Fine." Peggy hung up.

Peggy loved to hang up on him, especially when he called from the car. He figured she gambled that by the time he got back from his appointment, he'd have calmed down. Deep down, Tom knew to never underestimate the power of a secretary, even an average one like Peggy.

I should try to be nicer. Not lose my temper. Nah. Fuck it.

In forty minutes, traffic moved only six miles. With each passing moment, Tom's blood pressure surged. He heard a pounding in his ears and his clenched jaw sent pain crawling down the back of his neck and spine.

At last, the farm equipment turned off down an unmarked country lane, a cloud of brown dust left in its wake. Once the stalled traffic started moving, he arrived at Dick and Marge, a.k.a. "Tiny" Fester's house in ten minutes.

The Festers had lived in this same house for thirty-four years. Even after their sizable settlement, they opted to stay put in their modest three-bedroom rancher. Its most exceptional feature was its color, a faded cotton candy pink shade of aluminum siding.

The Festers spent most of their spare time in the backyard, splashing in their Olympic-sized, in-ground swimming pool. Other than drinking and smoking, it was their main source of entertainment. They used it from the first warm day in April well into October.

As soon as he opened his car door, Tom imagined he could smell the thick cigarette smoke that hung like a cloud all around the Festers' house. He walked up the front sidewalk and took a deep breath before ringing the doorbell.

Tiny Fester answered the door as she always did, with an unfiltered Pall Mall dangling from her lips. In her left hand, she held her favorite morning breakfast drink—tomato juice splashed into a tall glass of icy Budweiser.

"Hello, doll," she said to Tom. "Come on in. Your girl called and told us you were running late. How's about a beer?"

"Hi, Tiny," Tom said. He tried hard to sound pleasant, despite his dark mood. "Thanks, but it's a little early for me." Tom fake chuckled as he looked at the brown cuckoo clock on the wall. Only 10:30 A.M.

"Well, hell, son! It's five o'clock somewheres, I always say," Dick Fester cackled. He slowly made his way across the living room floor in his wheelchair. "Good to see ya, Tom!"

"Hey there, Dick," Tom said. "How're you feeling?"

"Full of piss and vinegar, same as always, son!" Dick said. "I'm just as ornery as a two-peckered rooster! Ha, ha, ha!" Dick laughed loudly at his joke, but stopped when a phlegm-rattled cough grabbed ahold of him. He coughed for what felt like two full minutes.

As they moved toward the dining room where they always held their meetings, Tiny offered Tom some iced-tea, his favorite. He accepted the glass and smiled at his hostess while he took a sip. Too bad it was sweet tea. He really preferred black, but he would never hurt Tiny's feelings. The painful memory of his day with the Stabs loomed fresh in his mind, and he was grateful for the hospitality.

The dining room, the most formal in the Fester's house, hadn't changed a bit over the years. Their elegant, although ancient dining room suite looked oddly out of place given the rest of the house.

Dick and Tiny considered their furniture fancy. A cut glass top protected the mahogany from wear and tear, and the formal cloth chairs were covered in cracked plastic, and yellowed with age. Burn marks from careless cigarette ashes spotted the green shag carpeting, a product of the early 1970s. Dusty venetian blinds, sticky with nicotine residue, remained closed always, although no neighbors lived nearby.

Maybe they're worried the sun will fade their furniture?

As if on cue, Dick wheeled himself over to the table and lit up a Pall Mall.

"Well, let's get this party started, Tom," he wheezed. "Tell me how much money I made last quarter."

Engulfed in the fresh cloud of smoke, Tom tried to take a deep breath before launching into his report. He discreetly removed two aspirin from the plastic pill case in his pocket and swallowed them with his tea.

While they made small talk, Tom asked about the Fester's two children and handful of grandchildren.

If they visit often, they're probably all asthmatics.

Tom always began his meetings by asking clients if they had any questions or concerns. Pleased with the performance of their accounts, Dick and Tiny rarely commented. He had them in a nice mix of blue-chip stocks, some bonds and a very safe amount of cash kept liquid. Just in case of emergencies.

"Hey, uh, Tom. What do you know about medical marijuana? Are people investin' in that shit? Is it somethin' we should be thinkin' about?" Dick dragged deeply on his Pall Mall and then coughed for an awkward amount of time.

"I'm sorry? What did you just say?"

"Dope. Pot. You know, Mary Jane! That's what we called it in the sixties! Come on, buddy, you know what I'm talkin' about! I figure with all these states makin' the shit legal—oh, I mean, medically necessary, or whatever they're callin' it—I mean, my God, there's gotta be a fortune t'be made. Rolling in the green! I'd say!" Again Dick laughed at his joke and coughed violently.

"Hmm. Well, Dick. That's an interesting idea." Tom smiled now, and paused for effect. He knew the perfect fund to suggest to the Festers.

The so-called Sin Fund had been around for a while, and stayed popular among his more open-minded clients. Although morally reprehensible to conservative clients, it had its charms for others: namely alcohol, tobacco, marijuana and the real prize: a brothel in Amsterdam called 'Wham-Bam Amsterdam'.

This fund remained recession-proof, and succeeded in almost any environment. When people were happy they drank to celebrate. But when people were sad or unemployed, or distressed in some other way, they also drank to kill the pain.

Now, when you talked about smoking, that hit a homerun too. All tobacco products proved so addictive, many users found it impossible to quit. And then the brothel! Sex never went out of style—legal or not. The pot thing kept growing in popularity, too, both literally and figuratively. Pure genius.

Tom launched into his explanation to the Festers and they were more than happy to purchase some of this fine stock fund. Tom promised to make the necessary changes to their account as soon as he got back to the office.

By the time he left, smoke oozed out of every pore in his body. His hair and clothes stank as if he had been in a smoky bar for a day and a half.

He climbed into his car, rolled down all the windows, opened the sunroof and started driving. Just out of sight of the house, he pulled over to the side of the road. He opened the trunk and whipped out a large spray bottle of Febreze, and began to spray his clothing. Frustrated, he looked down at his suit pants, and wished he could strip down to his boxers. *Too risky, even here in big-sky country.* He shrugged and sprayed his pants until he felt the liquid seep onto his skin. He didn't care if he returned to his office a damp, wrinkled mess. In fact, he doubted he had the gumption to go back there without changing his clothes altogether.

He cleaned up as much as possible, and got back on the road. A glance at his gas gauge revealed he needed a fill-up pronto. After a few minutes, he entered the tiny town of Blue Bell, a few miles north of the Maryland border. He remembered a Gutter's Gas Station & Food Market located somewhere on this road, so he forged ahead.

At last he spotted the Gutters, and pulled in to fill up his tank. Flimsy plastic bags covered the nozzles of many of the pumps. Frustrated, he circled in and around several before he found an available pump with the gas nozzle on the correct side. He refused to stretch the hose across the back of the car to reach the tank. Nothing dared scratch Tom's beloved Mercedes.

He swiped his credit card and filled up with the highest-octane fuel they offered, a medium grade. He reasoned he only needed enough to get back to civilization. As he pumped gas in his dress pants, wingtip shoes and wife-beater undershirt, he glanced across the parking lot and noticed something strapped to the roof of a small car. He stopped squeezing the nozzle and stared, not quite believing what he saw. He took a few steps to get a better look.

He saw it clearly now. The faded yellow Mazda sported a large dead pig strapped to its roof rack. It was white with several black splotches, and pink in all the right places. From where he stood, Tom surmised the pig, although uncovered, looked gutted. But its head remained attached. In an effort to keep his field of vision clear, the driver tied the head off the windshield, thus the hindquarters and legs draped over much of the back windshield. Tom continued to stare, open mouthed in disbelief.

Maybe I breathed in too much Febreze.

Tom finished pumping gas, grabbed the receipt and climbed into his car. His stomach growled and he realized he hadn't eaten anything yet.

Should I walk over to the store? Get a better look at the pig? Nah. I just need to get the hell out of this place.

He couldn't stop thinking about the hog as he drove away from the macabre mini-market. *Was it a real pig? Or a fake one? No, that's even weirder. Maybe the driver was headed to a pig roast, equipped with the main course?*

He looked at the dashboard clock and saw it had just turned two o'clock. No wonder his hands shook from hunger. He had intended to stop for lunch, but now he wanted to get home fast.

Starving, he rummaged around in his glove compartment, and found an ancient pack of Lance Crackers and a half pack of stale almonds. That would have to do for now.

He picked up the phone to call Peggy then changed his mind. He'd had enough madness for one day. God, he needed a drink. Badly. In fact, he hoped he could make the 20-minute drive to his house without one. Up ahead, he saw the signs for the expressway, so he pulled off to the shoulder of the road. He decided to call Peggy after all, picked up his phone and hit speed dial number three.

"Good afternoon, Mr. Frye's office," Peggy said.

"Hey, it's me," Tom said. "I'm going home for today. I'm not feeling very well."

"Well, that's just great, because Marcia Markel has been here for an hour and a half, waiting to see you. She says it's urgent. What shall I tell her?"

He realized instantly he needed to resign himself to another unpleasant task.

"Nobody says no to Marcia. Tell her I'll see her in twenty minutes," Tom said. "I just hope the Febreze worked its magic."

"No worries," Peggy said. "Standard just delivered your dry cleaning."

"Awesome," Tom said. "I'll see you soon."

God only knows what Marcia could possibly want. Seeing her is never a good thing.

As he continued on the drive back to his office, Tom puzzled over his changed attitude. *What's happened to my ambition? Is this a midlife crisis? I used to be optimistic. Laidback.*

He remembered the excitement and thrill of following the markets as a teenager in his economics classes, when the bug for the NYSE first bit him. It was too good to be true that you took cash, invested in somebody else's dream and made more money for yourself. It used to make his pulse race.

But not anymore.

The lure of becoming a financial advisor rooted itself in his fascination with the stock market. The action of the market portrayed Capitalism in its most raw form. It was pure. Not pure, though, were the humans who governed these markets. And time in the stock market wasn't measured in hours, days or weeks. It had its own timeframe.

After decades in existence, with its ups and downs, the highs and lows, the bull market versus the bear market, one thing stayed constant: it remained an unpredictable phenomenon. Why? Because the market was governed by human emotions, two very important and powerful ones: fear and greed.

Tom knew the beauty of the stock market lay in its potential to be a long-term wealth-creating factory for its investors. It paid for college, or the promise of a happy retirement; it also padded the pockets of greedy politicians. It exempted no one from its downfalls or its rewards. Even philanthropists benefitted when it helped them contribute to their favorite charities.

The secret revealed to Tom so long ago that still rang true today, was that every American had the chance to participate in this wealth-generating machine called the New York Stock Exchange. Everyone was welcome to the game.

When he got back to the office, Tom skipped the elevator and walked up the back stairs instead. He didn't want to risk seeing Marcia before he got cleaned up. Bone tired, he dreaded this unexpected intrusion. Conversations with her tended to be exhausting even on a good day. Anxiously he rubbed his hand across his face.

What does Marcia have in store for me today?

He found out soon enough.

CHAPTER FOUR

The parking garage stairs made it easy for Tom to sneak into his office. Undetected, he slipped into his private bathroom—one of the perks he earned as a senior vice president. The climb up four flights left him out of breath, but at least Peggy came through. She smuggled in a change of clothes and hung them on the back of the door. He showered, changed and got ready to meet with Marcia.

First he needed to assess the situation, so he turned on the surveillance camera that connected his office with the reception area. He saw Marcia, sighing and flipping through a magazine. She looked angry. Peggy continued to stall for time, so Tom paused to listen to their conversation on the intercom.

"Okay, Ms. Markel," Peggy said. "Tom should be here any minute."

"Finally," Marcia growled.

A self-proclaimed "bitch with a law degree," Marcia looked formidable in a black leather mini skirt and blazer, with thigh-high, stacked heel, black leather boots. *Like a scary dominatrix.* Pixie-short, highlighted hair and heavy makeup completed the look.

"Did you want anything while you wait? More coffee? Something to read?"

"No," Marcia said. "I think I need to find the restroom." Abruptly she got up and moved toward the ladies room in the lobby.

"Hmmph," Peggy said as she re-positioned herself behind the desk. Tom watched her pick up her cell.

Probably texting Derrick.

Tom finished getting ready, turned off the intercom and walked out to the reception area. Within a few minutes, Marcia stomped back and slapped her leather purse on the coffee table. It took her a moment to notice Tom standing there.

"Marcia," he said and reached out to shake her hand. "Sorry I kept you waiting so long. I wasn't expecting to see you today."

Marcia jumped to her feet, grabbed Tom and dragged him toward his office door. Then she stopped, and swung around to face him. Like a wolf stalking its prey, she sniffed. Tom's armpits grew damp. What was she doing? Marcia terrified him—as did most strong, outspoken women.

"Did you keep me waiting so you could take a *shower*? Didn't your secretary tell you this was an emergency?"

"Now Marcia, I ran into a problem at my last appointment, and I needed to get cleaned up." Tom wondered why he had volunteered that detail. *Damn nerves.*

Marcia rolled her eyes and then followed him into his office.

Still unnerved, he psyched himself to regain control.

Once inside, Marcia pushed Tom into his chair and then perched on top of his desk. She stared down into his eyes. The hair on the back of his neck stood on end.

"Tom, I needed to talk to you, and I couldn't risk doing it over the phone. I think my phones are tapped. In fact, I might have been followed here—I'm not sure." She paused, took a deep breath and drummed her fingernails. Faint beads of sweat dotted her upper lip.

For a moment, Tom said nothing and stared at his client. Tapped phones? Being followed? His pulse raced, but he forced his voice to sound calm. "Slow down," he said. "Tell me what happened. Start at the beginning."

Marcia got up and paced around the room. She picked up lamps, decorative pieces and the telephone. "Just looking for bugs, Tom," she said. "I can't be certain that they haven't infiltrated all of my contacts—especially my financial advisor. They've been looking for anything they can come up with—real or not. Hey. Start looking behind all those paintings and awards hanging on the wall too. You do that while I check everything on your desk."

"Marcia, you're not making any sense. Tell me what's happening? Please?"

Tom wanted to ignore her. Checking behind his wall hangings was absurd. He scanned the numerous plaques, awards and commendations he'd gathered from his years in the business: Volunteer of the Year for the Cray Chamber of Commerce, numerous Global International awards for superior performance, Chairman's Club Membership for Excellence from the Certified Financial Planning Association, and of course his college diploma, just to name a few.

Meanwhile, Marcia turned over his water bottle, mugs, pictures of his family, stacks of papers and books.

Annoyed, he steered her away from his desk. "No need to mess with this stuff. I really doubt there are any bugs among my personal belongings."

"Yeah, well, let's hope you're right, mister. I mean, I didn't want to come to you with this, but... well..." she glared at Tom, hesitating before finally adding, "I'm being blackmailed."

"Blackmail—you're positive?" A host of questions flooded his brain and he fired non-stop. "Marcia, who is it? Is it some thug, ex-con client just getting out of prison? Or, no, wait! Maybe it's the angry wife of someone you hooked up with? Is it someone you know?"

"I had no idea you thought so highly of me," Marcia said, clearly not amused. "No, it's nothing like that. It's just... well.... It's kind of hard to talk about—with you or anyone. I'm being accused—falsely accused, I might add—of some stuff, and I'm going to need to free up my assets. I need to hire an attorney," she laughed. "A really great, expensive attorney."

Marcia jumped up from the desk and circled around the office again. As she talked, she fluffed pillows and straightened pictures. She was acting nervous... and afraid. This woman ate napalm for breakfast. She practiced hand-to-hand combat with her karate instructor just for kicks. This woman loved to emasculate men.

Tom took a deep breath and tried to regain his focus. "Listen, Marcia. Anything you tell me is in confidence. You know that, and if you'd rather not disclose the nature of your problem, that's fine. But I have to caution you. You don't have a lot of liquid assets to draw from. Much of your wealth remains tied up in real estate—your law offices, the condo you bought your mother, your summer cottage on the Cape. All of those are heavily mortgaged, and you don't have a lot of equity in them yet. Frankly, you've just recently finished paying your college loans, and..."

"Just stop right there, champ," Marcia said. She put up her hand with a stopping motion. "Don't tell me that I don't have any money. Do you know how much I make? Five hundred bucks an hour, for chrissakes. I'm one of the top lawyers in this crappy little town!"

"All right, now, Marcia. Calm down. Yes, I know how much money you make, but what you earn and what you have available are two different issues. You spend a lot of money, and you haven't been great about saving lately..."

"What are you saying, Tom? Are calling me a spendthrift? Accusing me of not being fiscally responsible?"

Tom wanted to sound cheerful. Instead his voice cracked and warbled. "Let's start over. How much cash do you think you'll need? Then we can see how we can get it, okay?" He looked down and saw his fists were clenched at his sides.

"Don't patronize me, you little asshole! I'll carve you up and have you for my supper," Marcia seethed. "You better find me a million dollars, and find it quick, or I'm going to find a different financial advisor!"

Her eyes narrowed to squinty hard pebbles, and her face and hair looked sweaty. She collapsed into a chair, gasping as sobs wracked her shoulders.

Marcia Markel, crying?

"Jesus H. Christ!" Tom said and walked over to a small wooden credenza. Fiddling in his pocket, he pulled out his key ring and unlocked the cabinet. From inside he removed a bottle of very old Scotch. After splashing some of the expensive liquor into two glasses, he delivered the drinks and sat opposite his client.

"Here, have a drink. Let's try and go over what's happened." Tom tried to temper his tone, but the prospect of comforting Marcia scared the hell out of him.

"What about my IRA? Can't I borrow against it, or my assets, or something?" She wailed now, streams of black mascara dripping down her face.

"Marcia, tell me what's going on or I can't help you." He looked at the pathetic woman in front of him, wondering what she might confide.

Marcia sniffed and began, "Well, I suppose it goes back to a case I took a few years ago. In fact, you probably remember hearing about it? The local wrestling coach accused of inappropriate conduct with a few of the boys on his team?"

Tom nodded. *Holy shit. It can't be.*

Marcia continued.

"Well, the one kid—there were actually two brothers, both on the varsity wrestling team—but anyway the younger one, Alex, started to have terrible pain during one of his 'private' wrestling practice sessions with Coach Leon Burke—you know the name?"

She paused here and waited for acknowledgment. Distracted, Tom managed to nod then motioned for her to continue.

Oh my God. Burke. Leon? The son of Jack Burke? Oh shit. No.

"So anyway," Marcia continued, "this coach, gym teacher, whatever the fuck he is, decided to drive the kid to the ER himself. Didn't check with the parents, just scooped the kid and his brother up and drove to the hospital."

Marcia paused and threw up her hands in disgust.

"He suspected the kid might have a hernia. That was his excuse. And he didn't want to be blamed for anything. So he took both kids over to the ER, assuming the older brother would call the parents. But no one contacted the parents until hours later."

Tom puzzled over this unlikely scenario. *How could this happen with all the HIPAA rules and regulations today? Who would do something so stupid?* He realized Marcia had started talking again so he tried hard to concentrate.

"Well, I guess the older brother, Tony, eventually called the parents, who hustled over there. Coach Leon stayed with Alex, who screamed non-stop, worried about his nuts. Thought his junk was broken or something."

Jesus, I wrestled for years and never heard a story like this.

"So the coach decided to have a gander in the exam room, while they waited for the doc and the parents. I mean he actually started to grope the kid! Told him if he could still get a hard-on, everything was fine!"

Marcia paused to catch her breath. Tom listened in disbelief. *How do you figure into this whole nightmare, Marcia?*

"Just think about it. You've got a kid in severe pain, and then this jerk starts to beat him off. In the fucking hospital exam room. The kid started to scream for help, so the coach took off. By the time anyone got there Leon was long gone."

Marcia took another gulp from the glass of Scotch and continued.

"It ended up the kid had a twisted testicle, or something. Lost a nut. I don't know if that had anything to do with wrestling, or not. But the coach was in deep shit. He violated all sorts of school rules. Not to mention the ethical complications. The parents tried to keep it hush-hush but the story exploded on social media. Rumors were flying and the school board flipped out."

Tom interrupted, "But weren't they minors? How could it not be in the paper, Marcia?"

She looked annoyed by his interruption. "Well, the bastard never did have to go to court and the school district settled very quickly with the parents to keep it out of the news. The parents have a bunch of other kids I think, some pompous banker and his flaky wife. They didn't give a shit about their son. They wanted the cash, and they wanted Leon fired. Do you remember hearing any of this?"

How could I forget? My client's son...

"Oh, yeah. I remember." Tom took another sip of Scotch and contemplated whether he'd need a refill. "Wait a minute. Banker's kids? Wrestlers? What's the last name?"

"Name? Sajak. Frank is the dad's name."

Oh this keeps getting better. I know that pompous prick Frank from the Cray Chamber of Commerce. "Huh. You don't say. That name sounds familiar."

Marcia glared at him, anxious to finish her story. "Anyway, the coach waited a few months, and tried to resume contact with the boys. It turns out they loved my ads on television. You know, my 'Med Mal with Marcia' campaign? They called me for a consult. Those poor kids, so embarrassed people would think they were gay. Let me clarify, I *know* they're not. I got to know these boys."

Tom nodded again while Marcia took another sip of her Scotch and blew her nose into a tissue.

"They wanted to come in and talk to me privately, after hours. You know, to see what I thought. Well, typically I only deal in medical malpractice, but I was intrigued. They looked cute, and I needed to decide if they had grounds to file harassment charges, stalking, anything."

Tom scowled and looked annoyed.

"I didn't know yet if this warranted medical malpractice. Plus, the hospital left the kid alone with the coach until his parents arrived. Get my drift?"

Marcia paused and took another long deep breath. Tom nodded, rolled his eyes again and signaled her to continue.

"So, the boys—Tony and Alex—they came over a couple of nights after my staff left. They didn't want anyone to see them and leak it to the press. So we had a meeting of the minds, so to speak." Marcia stared at Tom and waited for a reaction.

"That's it?" Tom asked. "They hung out with you a few times while you offered them counsel, end of story?"

Marcia said nothing and continued to stare.

Then, it dawned on him. *Oh. My. God.* It took a moment before he could speak. "Are you saying what I think you're saying? Are you telling me that you slept with these boys?"

"Now just hold your horses, mister. I didn't say anything of the sort. Therein lies the problem, asshole! Their parents claim I lured them to my office after hours, plied them with booze and took advantage of them—all under the guise of coaching them. I'm ruined."

Tom glared at her. "What do you mean, the parents? What do the parents have to do with it? How old are these kids anyway? Didn't their parents have to come along to your office? Can they even drive yet?"

"Oh yeah, well, see that's the thing," Marcia said. "Only minors need parental consent. They didn't need to tell their parents anything—just dealt with me directly. For advice, I mean."

Tom felt the bile rising in his throat. He remembered rumors circulating a few years ago that Marcia spent a lot of extra time 'mentoring' some of her law clerks. Young, handsome men; Harvard graduates. Marcia handled the merchandise. And enjoyed it.

Tom rose from his chair, downed the remaining Scotch in his glass and looked down at Marcia. As he took in her tear-stained face, it dawned on him. "So seriously. Do the parents think you molested the boys? Took advantage of them sexually? Exploited them for your own sick pleasure?"

"Something like that, yes," she whispered. "They're threatening to go to the press if I don't give them each a half a million dollars." She looked up at him and batted her smeared black eyes. "All I wanted to do was help, Tom. That's all."

"Marcia, did you have sex with these boys, with both of those underage kids? For God's sake, how could you?"

"Tom, stop! You don't understand," she said. "They were over eighteen. I mean I didn't sleep with both of them at the same time or anything."

Tom couldn't help himself from cringing.

She grabbed her elbows and hugged herself tightly. "I tried to act like a good friend. With that crazy coach trying to get into their pants, they needed to confirm their sexuality. They wanted an experienced older woman—you know, a cougar-type to take them under her wing and show them a few things." Marcia squared her shoulders and sat up tall. "Really—it was almost... educational."

To Tom, it looked as though a wave of calm washed over her. She stood up to smooth her skirt, then walked over to his desk and pulled out a compact and powder puff from her purse. She peered into the mirror and applied powder to her nose and chin. After primping, she looked over at him and smiled.

"Tom," she said sweetly, walking back toward him, "you were right. I should've told you the truth to begin with. Of course, I know I can trust you. I know you'll help me. What a relief!"

Tom looked at Marcia, his client for over ten years. He took a deep breath and then blew it out in a big puff. Now he saw the truth. He couldn't continue this relationship. Not only did it undermine his credibility, but it also crossed a moral boundary. He couldn't work with a child molester. It made him physically ill, and went against everything he believed in. He couldn't represent this woman anymore.

"Marcia," he said, "I heard rumors for years that you liked young men, and I always figured it for gossip. Just idle gossip from insecure male colleagues who coveted your success. Never in a million years did I imagine you capable of taking advantage of *minors*." Tom cleared his throat and continued, his voice rising in pitch and volume as he pointed his finger toward the door. "Get out," he said. "Get out right now. We're done."

"What do you mean, we're done? Nobody's done with anything here."

He pulled her by the wrist toward the door. "No, Marcia. Wrong," he said. "We're done. You're fired. I'm firing you. I don't ever want to talk to you again. Find yourself another financial advisor. We're through. I mean it. I can't be a part of this crap. As soon as you leave, I'm calling the firm's legal team to make sure I file a full disclosure with them. I can't be associated with someone like you. Find another advisor and I'll work out the details with them. Goodbye."

He opened the door and nudged a stunned Marcia out into the lobby.

"Peggy, will you call security please? Ms. Markel needs an escort out of the building." For once, Tom's tone of voice and stern glance dictated authority. Peggy picked up the phone on her desk and dialed building security.

Marcia turned her back on them both and rooted around inside her clothes. For a moment Tom thought she would flash him. But instead she turned around, pulled a tiny container of mace from her bra, and aimed.

It hit Tom straight in the face. The vile liquid sprayed into his eyes, nose and mouth in one quick motion. He immediately dropped and writhed on the ground, clawing at his face and screaming.

Marcia walked over to where he lay and assessed her work. She smiled.

He covered his face with his hands. Tears and snot ran down the front of his shirt and tie, and he struggled to spit the mace out of his mouth onto the floor.

Marcia loomed over him, casting a towering black shadow. "No one fires me, asshole," she said. "Ever. You better remember that."

Unfortunately, with Tom's blurred vision, he never saw her draw her high-heeled boot back and kick him squarely in the balls. The impact lifted him several inches off the floor, and knocked his head against the cold marble tile.

Marcia flicked imaginary dust off her jacket, and squared her shoulders. Tom lay motionless on the floor.

"Oh my God! You killed him," screamed Peggy.

"No. I think he just fainted," said Marcia. "But you might want to call 911 just in case."

Like a robot, Peggy reached for the phone, her gaze fixed on Marcia. Within moments, two security guards arrived with weapons drawn. When they spotted Tom thrashing on the floor, they rushed toward him.

Marcia broke into a run, but one of the guards grabbed her by the sleeve, holding tight while she squirmed.

"Hold it right there, ma'am," said the guard. "I'm afraid you're not going anywhere." He pushed Marcia into a nearby chair. "Stay right there," he added.

Tom moaned and writhed while Peggy summarized the assault for the security guards. Together they managed to rouse him with smelling salts and tried to prop him up against a sofa with some pillows. Soon an ambulance arrived and the paramedics began treatment. They cleaned off his face and lifted him onto the couch.

After a few minutes, Tom could gradually see again. Before long, the Cray Police Department showed up and arrested Marcia. He heard her muffled screams and curses echo throughout the lobby as they dragged her off.

"Feel better, Mr. Frye," a young police officer yelled, waving his chubby hand in the air. "We'll contact you at home to get your statement."

Still dazed and in pain, Tom waved weakly to the cop. He adjusted the icepack on his crotch and asked the paramedic for some aspirin.

"Sir, I think you're gonna need something stronger than that," said the paramedic. "But don't you worry. In a day or two you'll be good as new. How about if we give you a shot—no, no, not there—a shot for the pain... and the swelling—sorry, man. It'll help you relax. Just, you won't be able to drive yourself home. Can we call your wife to pick you up?"

Tom nodded. Peggy called Vicky and explained the situation while the paramedics injected the shot, and after checking his vital signs, gave him the green light to go home and rest.

Peggy waved goodbye to the paramedics and sat beside her boss on the couch to wait for Vicky. "That EMT was so cute, wasn't he?"

Tom rolled his eyes in disgust. "Really, Peggy? Flirting with the paramedics? Jesus."

Peggy shrugged and smirked. "Yeah, well, anyway, Tom. What happened in there with Marcia?" He threw her a dirty look and said nothing. "Tom?" she asked again.

"I'm too tired to talk about it. I just wanna go home."

"Well, good for you," Peggy said patting his shoulder. For once she was not being sarcastic.

CHAPTER FIVE

Tom remembered little about the drive home from work. After Vicky picked him up, he managed to stay awake long enough to explain what happened. Exhausted, he walked through the door, collapsed on the couch and passed out. When Vicky managed to get him to bed, he slept for twenty-four hours.

He finally woke with his tongue fuzzy and his mouth dry. As he got out of bed and made his way to the bathroom, he expected worse pain, even bracing himself for equipment failure, but everything still worked. Thank God the paramedics put ice on his balls right away. *Marcia must not have kicked me as hard as I thought.* He threw on sweat pants and an old tee shirt, then made his way down the steps and into the kitchen.

"Hello," he said to no one in particular. No answer. A little louder he yelled again, "Hello... anybody home?" Still no one answered him. Alone, thank God. He headed for the fridge and grabbed a cold beer.

Where was everyone? His wife's Subaru sat in the garage. But then he noticed the kid's car, an old Nissan, was gone. Dazed, he carried his beer into the family room and sank into the comfy chintz sofa. He chugged the cold brew and then leaned his head back. Still groggy from the shot, he dozed. A nap was just what he needed.

After twenty minutes, he woke to find his wife's pretty face poised over him, her brows knitted together in worry.

"Tom? Honey? Are you all right? How do you feel?"

Vicky always worried, whether she had a reason or not. Always.

"What? No, I'm fine. Better than expected. Just tired," he said. "Where were you guys?"

"Out running a few errands, nothing exciting," Vicky said. "Giving Sophie a chance to practice her parallel parking."

From the kitchen, voices rose. "Mom!" screamed Sophie, "Jane is being a pig again! She ate all the pizza!"

"Honestly, Mom, Sophie and her creepy little friends scarfed all of it yesterday. I only had one piece. I couldn't stand to be around them. All they do is giggle and whisper." Jane munched on the slice as she walked out of the kitchen.

"Mom. Make her stop! I hate her," Sophie said, losing this battle to her older, quicker sister.

Tom stood and wrapped his arms around his youngest child. "Soph, why don't you call that pizza joint downtown and order us a couple pizzas for tonight?"

Sophie squealed. "Excellent idea, Daddy," she said and squirmed out of his embrace. From the kitchen Tom heard her call Papa Dino's.

"Problem solved, I'm a genius!" Tom said, as he coaxed a smile from Vicky.

"Well, genius," she replied, "do you really feel well enough to head over to Papa D's to pick up our pizza?"

"I guess so. Sophie will have to drive. I drank a few beers earlier."

With that out in the open, Tom seized the opportunity to drink another. He hobbled to the refrigerator to grab one.

Anyway, Sophie needs the practice, so she'll be the one behind the wheel.

Armed with her driver's permit, Sophie never passed up an opportunity to drive anywhere. But as Tom downed another beer, Vicky's smile twisted into a scowl. She said nothing. She didn't need to. Before she changed her mind, he made a beeline for the car.

Sophie climbed behind the wheel and careened out of the driveway too fast. Tom gasped and braced his hands against the dashboard. Oblivious, she drove and chattered nonstop with the radio blaring. He turned it down and wished he had stayed home. But he wanted to teach Sophie to drive. Vicky, a terrible backseat driver, had relinquished the job immediately.

Although Sophie did well enough for a beginner, she lacked confidence. In the meantime, their car insurance premiums had skyrocketed, and Jane's trio of accidents last year made him anxious.

When they arrived at Papa Dino's about five minutes later, he and Sophie walked into the shop. A long line formed at the counter, which annoyed him. His family liked this place because it had good food, clean bathrooms, and friendly staff. The longtime owners, a nice couple with grown kids, let the teenagers hang out and put money in the jukebox. But Tom preferred Papa Dino's takeout. He loathed paper plates, plastic silverware and the company of love-struck teenyboppers. Plus, they didn't sell alcohol, and he couldn't have fun without it these days.

Is my drinking a problem? He dismissed the thought immediately.

As they stood in line, Tom sighed. He stared off into the distance and ignored the ruckus, until a tap on the shoulder startled him.

There stood Walter, a guy he knew from high school. They had worked together as landscapers at the Country Bumpkin Nursery. For years it had been a mom-and-pop landscaping joint operated out of a shack. They sold tomatoes and planted rosebushes and hedges for little old ladies and the regular customers without a green thumb. The Bumpkin had grown over the years when the owner Dennis Bumpkin added lawn furniture, reflecting balls, garden gnomes and the like.

Tom had worked there all through high school and college, and learned a lot about the garden business. Most of it he enjoyed, with the exception of the annual trip out to Dennis'

Christmas Tree Farm. For three weeks straight he trimmed trees. Alone. The work was slow, tedious, and fell during the hottest part of the summer.

But every spring now, Tom and Vicky waited impatiently for the weather to warm up enough to start their garden. Herbs, vegetables and flowers overflowed in their cart, and created hours of work for both of them. Since the employees at the Country Bumpkin recognized them on sight, what should have been a quick trip usually lasted for hours. Some of the same employees had worked with Tom, and enjoyed a chance to chat. But it was worth it. Their vegetable and flower gardens were the envy of the neighborhood.

Not only had his job at the Bumpkin made him into a lifelong gardener, it taught him the importance of building relationships. Dennis, a bizarre man, fell into dark abusive moods, and yelled at his employees without provocation. But other times, he acted oddly philanthropic. Tom thought him a strange mixture of stubborn Pennsylvania Dutch mixed with cheapskate entrepreneur. Although he justified underpaying his employees, he claimed to be a great Christian, and donated large sums of money to the Catholic Church.

Tom had been working there about eighteen months when he received a call from the Department of Labor. The agent on the phone asked him if he was a "farm worker." Tom laughed and replied that he was a store clerk and part-time landscaper. Little did Tom know, Dennis took advantage of his youngest employees and classified them as farm workers to pay them lower wages. At fifteen, Tom missed the irony. But a few months later, he received a check for several hundred dollars— a remittance for being underpaid by about eighty cents an hour. That money went towards a new bike to get him back and forth to work.

Tom shook hands with Walter and introduced his daughter Sophie. As they greeted one another, Tom noticed Walter's large calloused palms, rough from a lifetime spent in manual labor. Funny, because now Tom's own hands felt as smooth as a baby's butt from years in corporate finance. Now, if he wanted to, he could pay someone else to do his landscaping. But he refused to give it up. It was his refuge, and the only place he could lose himself.

Walter was a pleasant, easy-going fellow who loved to gossip as much as an old lady and looked the same as ever. Well over six feet, only the lines on his face and a small smattering of grey in his hair gave away his age. He looked happy to see Tom and rattled off familiar names, but most stories still focused around Dennis. Like old times, the boss stalked his employees, followed them to job sites and terrorized them with low pay.

Tom remembered multiple times when a crew, inches from a finished project, found themselves faced with an angry Dennis. He picked apart the landscaping work, commanded plants be dug up and replanted elsewhere, or claimed the wrong plants had been installed.

Tom nodded in agreement while Walter chattered, and thought about the last time he'd seen Dennis at the nursery. Only a month ago, Dennis barreled over to where he and Vicky were examining roses bushes and demanded Tom provide investment ideas. *Typical Dennis, always trying to get free advice.* Dennis also criticized Tom's car. *"What's that? Your midlife crisis, Frye?"* He thought everyone should own a truck. And if you lacked the sensibility to own your own, you sure as hell shouldn't continue to expect free delivery from the Bumpkin.

Walter interrupted Tom's train of thought. "You should stop into the store more, man, I know he'd really appreciate a visit. Believe it or not, I think he's a big fan of yours. Always talking about what a big shot you turned out to be, and that he gave you your first job. You know Dennis. That SOB is always taking credit for things he had nothing to do with whatsoever." Walter glanced over to where Sophie stood tapping her foot, arms crossed across her chest. "Oh, hey, man, it looks like your daughter is giving you the evil eye. Your order is probably ready. You better get going."

Tom spotted Sophie near the cash register, impatience written all over her face.

"Yeah, the kid's always hungry. Well, good to see you again, man. Take it easy."

Tom slapped Walter on the back and walked up to the counter to pay. Sophie grabbed the two pizza boxes, and they headed for the car.

The slight beer buzz from earlier disappeared during the drive home. When Sophie hit a pothole, he slapped the dashboard and winced at the pain in his crotch. Cranky and tired, he attempted to readjust himself in the passenger seat. Sophie remained silent as she kept her eyes focused on the road.

Tom replayed the office scene over and over in his head, finally facing the truth. Marcia had bullied and assaulted him. Even worse, he knew it wasn't over. Marcia never went away quietly. He imagined she'd probably try to sue him. She was an attorney after all, and a humiliated one, so that made sense. And she'd been arrested. Regardless, Peggy had witnessed the whole thing, so that worked in his favor.

Let her sue, and good riddance. She never listened to any of my advice anyway, and she spent way too much money.

Still, no matter how he rationalized it, Tom didn't relish the idea of being sued.

Although he'd never mismanaged Marcia's money—or anyone else's for that matter—he wouldn't put it past her to lie and make up something unscrupulous. He decided to review all his client notes on Monday, and double-check his records. Luckily, Peggy had sat in on many of their meetings. Marcia frequently needed something notarized or copied, and in truth, Tom had avoided being alone with her whenever possible.

Sophie parked and carried the pizza boxes to the kitchen counter while Tom headed straight to the fridge for another beer. Pizza seemed like the last thing he was in the mood for.

Vicky glared at him and raised a well-groomed dark eyebrow. He pretended not to notice. The girls grabbed plates and loaded up slices. Tom sat drinking his beer as the two of them headed off into the family room to watch TV and gorge.

Vicky continued staring at him as she took a small deliberate bite from her pizza. Tom refused to make eye contact, and instead peeled the label from his bottle. As she always did, Vicky took a stack of paper napkins and blotted the top of the slice to absorb extra grease and save calories. When she finished, she washed her hands at the sink and turned to face Tom again.

Hands on her hips, she said, "So. Are we ready to talk about this?"

"Talk about what?" Tom said.

"Really? About that woman attacking you? The mace? The kicking you in the... I mean for God's sake, Thomas. What the hell happened there at your office yesterday?"

Tom sighed and chugged the rest of his beer. Vicky looked like she wanted to comment, but restrained herself, even while she watched him walk back to the fridge and grab another Heineken. He popped the top with the opener from the drawer and tossed it and the bottle cap onto the kitchen counter.

"Tom?"

"Stop. Stop. Stop! Don't go there. I'm not in the mood to discuss this right now, Vicky. It's under control. Don't worry about it."

"Stop? Don't worry about it?" She lowered her voice slightly, "Are you fucking kidding me? Goddammit, Tom, you will *not* speak to me like this. How dare you?" Her face flushed with anger and her hands shook when she put down the plate.

"Vick, I'm sorry. Client confidentiality, and all that bullshit. You know I can't talk about this with you. The woman is messed up. I fired her. She got pissed. That's all you need to know. The less you know, the better. Trust me."

"Confidentiality, my ass! No, Tom. You should trust *me*. You can't shut me out like this. This isn't fair."

"Vick. No. It's not fair. But I'm trying to protect you."

"Huh, that's a joke, right? Protect me? Really? You can't exclude me. I won't let you." She paused briefly to brush her long bangs back from her face. "But let me say this, if you don't want to talk about it tonight, fine. I get it. But you damn well better to be willing to share some more details about this with me tomorrow. I mean it."

Vicky grabbed her plate, poured herself a glass of wine and joined the girls in the family room. From the kitchen, he heard the muffled drone of canned television laughter. *Seinfeld, no doubt, but I'm not in the mood to laugh.*

He grabbed a slice of pizza and his beer, and moved to the kitchen table to read yesterday's *Wall Street Journal*. He perused the headlines, but retained nothing. He knew Vicky was right. He had shut out his family, especially her.

But I don't think she gets it. What I go through at work— professionally, mentally, physically. Why am I drinking so much? Why can't I take back control of my own life?

Something was missing and very wrong. As he sat at the kitchen table and looked out the window at the twilight summer sky, he felt the ache of loneliness. It was a beautiful night, breezy and warm, but not overly humid. Just like the summers he'd spent as a kid, hanging out down at the creek with his friends. Hours spent swinging from the rope on that old oak tree, and then exploding into the cold water. They dove off what the kids had called "the cliffs," a high rock formation along the top of the creek scary enough to put your heart in your stomach when you jumped.

He wished for the days when he had felt fearless and brave and courageous. Not like the frustrated, sulking defensive man he had become. He realized then what he needed to do. Tomorrow. Yes, tomorrow he needed to go the river.

CHAPTER SIX

Late Sunday afternoon, as soon as Vicky and the girls left to go shopping, Tom headed out to the river. He needed some time alone, and the Susquehanna would provide a balm for his frazzled nerves.

He made the short drive and relished the river's scent of fish and mud and life and death. Tom didn't own a boat and he wasn't a fisherman, but he loved hearing the rush of the current.

He parked in a gravel lot and headed down a steep embankment toward the river's edge. As he walked, he marveled at the native plants growing all around him. Wild daisies and lilies with bright orange faces moved in the breeze. Lush ferns hidden from the sun peeked out under tall pines and oak trees. He trudged on and soon found himself facing the water.

A crudely constructed tire swing hung from an enormous weeping willow, looking as if it might take you to the water's edge with enough momentum. He contemplated hopping on, but at his age, his tire swing days had passed.

Instead he kicked off his sandals, and wriggled his feet as they sank into the muddy riverbank. His toes traveled over sharp stones and broken mussel shells. The murky brown water slipped against his bare feet.

Tom walked to one of the large rocks that lined the river's edge and sat perched like a ruffled bird. *God, I need new clients if I'm going to stay in this business.* Even with Marcia gone, he still had a slew of others he wanted to fire. Like his hairline, his patience had receded and his book of business needed a manicure.

I really need a vacation. But at least I promised Vicky I'd go plant shopping at the Country Bumpkin on Friday.

The pressure mounted every year to find new business. Since Lance hadn't brought in any new clients for years, and saw no reason to start now, this task fell to Tom. Lance worked only three or four days a week and left early. When he did come into work, his voice carried through the whole office and disrupted everyone.

Referrals had dropped off too. Jim Doyle, his best source, hadn't sent him any lucrative clients of late. Entrenched in a third divorce, Jim had little time to practice law—let alone make legitimate referrals.

Tom's firm required a minimum of a million dollars in assets to sign a client. With all the work he put into an initial analysis of assets, liquidity, stocks, income, savings, and debt, it didn't make sense if profit wasn't on the horizon.

Tom started to splash his feet again.

Too bad I never took up fishing. It would've been a good way to pass the time. He remembered he and Vicky bringing the girls down to the river for weekend picnics. They'd skip stones and hike the trails.

As he splashed, he noticed something weaving and bobbing toward him in the water. The sun glinted on it, making tiny rainbows alternate with flashes of black. As it moved closer, Tom realized it was an empty bottle of Jack Daniels, rotating and spinning with the current. When it floated close enough to his rock perch, he reached down and plucked it from the water.

Hmmm, cap's on and everything. And the label is still attached.

He examined the weathered bottle, and then realized it contained a folded piece of paper. When he turned the bottle upside down, the paper inside slid below its neck.

Back near the shore, he grabbed a long, thin stick and got the paper close enough to reach it with his fingers. With some careful maneuvering, he pulled the tiny scroll out for inspection.

Tom wiped his muddy hands on his khaki shorts, now spotted with dirt and flecks of mud. He opened the creased, three-holed, college-ruled notebook paper, his heart racing with anticipation and excitement.

Maybe it's a love letter or a suicide note. As he unfolded the dirty sheet, his heart sank at the singular message:

Asshole.

Wow, really? Are you fucking serious? Who goes to the trouble to take an empty bottle, and stuff it with a note that says 'asshole'? Jesus!

Disgusted, he crumpled up the page and prepared to hurl the bottle back into the river, but then stopped and decided against it.

I can't litter.

Instead he folded the note and stuck it back inside the bottle. With the cap replaced, Tom and his new souvenir walked back to the rock.

"Why would anyone do this?" he said aloud. "I mean seriously... maybe it was some kid, or some sicko with nothing better to do. Or... maybe God is trying to tell me something!" He turned the bottle over and over in his hands. *Hmmm, this has potential to be an interesting marketing concept.*

He scratched his head and watched the boats floating in the distance. Then, like a flash, it came to him. *What if I wrote up a brief bio, attached my business card and some flashy statistics that would appeal to the free-spirited, boater types?* It was ingenious, this new idea, and a fantastic way to reach potential new clients. *But what would the Fish and Game Commission have to say? Well, I can worry about that later.*

When he got home, he grunted to his family in the kitchen and ran straight for his office.

He had barely googled "environmental hazards," when Vicky interrupted. "What in the world are you doing? And why does it smell like old creek water in here? Eew!" She held her nose, and fanned the air in front of her face for effect.

"Not creek water," said Tom. "I drove to the river to do a little thinking, and I came up with a great marketing idea for getting new business."

He explained his epiphany about the message in the bottle. Tom jumped up and handed her the rough outline he had sketched on some scratch paper at his desk. "Here, Vick. Check this out!"

Vicky took one look at the paper in his hand, and then stared at him in disbelief. "You're kidding, right? You'd be arrested for littering. Have you lost your mind?"

She grabbed the piece of paper, crumpled it into a ball, and tossed it into the trashcan. Her face flamed red, and her eyes looked wild. Tom knew this look, and it wasn't good.

His wife stood over him and yanked the laptop toward her. She read for a few moments before slamming it shut, then tucked it under her arm and turned to face him.

"Honey, I know you've been under a lot of pressure, but you can't be serious about this. Why would you think this cockamamie idea would work? Have you lost your mind?" Vicky paused for a minute then added, "I don't think I even know you anymore."

Tom opened his mouth to offer an explanation, but decided against it. He offered a pathetic shrug instead.

Vicky continued, "You need to get away from work for a while." She stepped back and assessed him. "Just look at you. You came in here dripping muddy water and dirt all over the floor. Either take a vacation or get to the doctor ASAP. You need help."

While his wife ranted, Tom's mind raced. He realized this idea had been ridiculous, but he needed something different to jumpstart his business. And his enthusiasm. Most of his clients were bat-shit crazy, or old as dirt and one heartbeat away from dying. Plus everyone feared the unstable markets.

Not that long ago, it gave Tom a rush to snag a new client. But now, all of his hard work went unrewarded. He waited around, sometimes for months, for people to decide if they wanted to become clients. Or if they hired him, they complained about the fees, or demanded daily updates on their accounts. Everyone wanted to play day trader now. People thought he had nothing better to do all day than scream "buy" or "sell" to imaginary Wall Street traders.

Tom imagined they had no idea about the research he pored over, or the time he put into personalizing their accounts. Plus the weird logic clients used for picking stocks—like the Stabs and their Swedish Fish...

He thought about a client who wanted to buy stock in "Wendy's" because his granddaughter liked their hamburgers. Another couple wanted him to rent a U-Haul to help them move. *Seriously?*

Clients called him day or night on his cell. Nothing was sacred to these people. He was merely a pawn in his own life. Vicky was right. He needed to stop the madness.

The following week was already booked solid. He and Lance were heading down to Georgia to see one of their most bizarre clients, Pastor Bob Raddison and his dingy wife, Babs. As soon as Tom got back from this business trip though, he'd plan a weekend getaway to clear his head. He only had to get through this trip with Lance first.

"Vick," he said, "you're absolutely right. I'm so tired, that's all. After the Georgia trip next week, we'll go somewhere, just the two of us." He grabbed her and gave her a big hug. "Longwood Gardens? Like I promised?"

Vicky smiled, but pulled out of his embrace and wrinkled her nose. "Okay, good," she said. "Now, will you please get cleaned up before dinner? You stink."

"Sure. Right behind you."

Her good humor restored, Vicky left Tom's office. He followed close behind, but not before pausing long enough to snatch his diagram of the bottle advertisement out of the trashcan. He smiled, folded it, and put it in his back pocket.

CHAPTER SEVEN

Tom knelt on the hardwood floor of La Bohème, and grimaced as he tried to listen to Pastor Bob. Tonight he found himself forced into publicly giving thanks to the Lord at one of the finest restaurants in Blue Ridge, Georgia. He shifted his weight, but to no avail. Kneeling hurt his knees, and he couldn't concentrate. But as usual, clients got what they wanted.

He stole a sideways slit of a glance at his partner, Lance, and stifled a laugh. A chubby, previously athletic rugby-type, Lance balanced on one knee and held tight to the edge of the heavy mahogany table.

The irony of the situation loomed large for Tom. Here in the heart of the Blue Ridge Mountains, he was groveling on hands and knees to secure a deal with yet another oddball client. Pastor Bob Raddison, a man of the cloth, entrepreneur and professional blabbermouth, rambled on and on. His tremulous tenor voice rose and fell, subtle as a rollercoaster.

"Dear Lord, thank you for this day, splendid in its uniqueness, and rich in its many gifts to us, your lowly servants. Thank you, Lord, for this opportunity to break bread with our traveling friends, Tom and Lance, who pause to dine with us in this place, and..."

The financial advisors exchanged eye rolls, anxious for the prayer to conclude.

Pastor Bob took a deep breath and continued, "Dear Lord, please bless our sister, Babs—your lovely and graceful servant—

as we await her arrival, to join us for a feast of thanksgiving and gratuity. And Lord, keep us ever vigilant as we await your Second Coming, when we will meet you face to face, soul to soul, heart to heart, in the final reckoning hour. Where we will rejoice in the faithful and mourn the brothers and sisters who failed to head the warning call of the Gospel!"

Tom fought the urge to crack his knuckles and punctuate the sanctimonious rant.

"Bless us Lord, as we break bread together... the humble and the faithful who await your coming: 'But of that day and hour knoweth no man, no, not the angels of heaven but my Father only. But as the days of Noah were, so shall also the coming of the Son of man be. For as in the days that were before the flood they were eating and drinking, marrying and giving in marriage, until the day Noah entered into the ark...'"

Tom's mind continued to drift as the catechism continued. *Do they give classes in biblical psychobabble? Is this a teachable skill?*

"...And knew not until the flood came, and took them all away; so shall also the coming of the Son of man be. Then shall two be in the field; the one shall be taken, and the other left. Two women shall be grinding at the mill; the one shall be taken, and the other left."

Pastor Bob let out a heavy gasp with the final proclamation. "Watch therefore: for ye know not what hour your Lord doth come." A heavy pause filled the air between the three men. "Gentleman, I give you the Holy Gospel, according to St. Matthew, chapter 24 verses 36-42," sighed Bob.

"Amen?" piped up a troubled Lance from the floor. "Jeez, I hate to interrupt, but I really gotta get to the can..."

Tom whipped around and glared at his partner.

But Bob smiled and waved the go ahead. Tom rolled his eyes as Lance sprinted off to the restroom. *Jeez, I've never seen Lance move so fast.*

When Tom got up from the floor, he strained to focus in the dark restaurant. Something under the corner of a nearby table caught his eye. He needed a closer look, so he bent down and retied his shoe.

Oh, shit.

On the floor at a table against the wall, Tom saw the mouse. A dead one, captured in a glue trap like a sticky coffin.

Holy hell, this is a five-star restaurant.

He sat up too fast and hit his head on the heavy edge of the table. "Ow, jeez, sorry. Guess I'm tired from traveling."

His head throbbed, but he forced a smile and flashed his perfect white teeth. He couldn't picture eating dinner with a dead mouse so close to his Italian loafers.

As he struggled to get comfortable, Tom caught the eye of a small boy, playing with a couple of Matchbox cars at a table across the room. The little boy ran cars up and down his mother's arm. When he ran the racecar up into his mother's tidy hairdo, she shooed him away, and banished him to the floor.

The boy plopped down and crashed his toy cars off the chair onto the carpeting. Tom watched him play, and nodded appropriately and smiled at his client. Anything was better than listening to Pastor Bob's boring stories about Blue Ridge parish life.

For crying out loud, why didn't the parents think to bring along crayons and a coloring book? My kid wouldn't be crawling all over this floor.

"I apologize, Tom. I can't imagine what's keeping Babs," said Bob. "She prides herself on punctuality. Always."

"Oh, no problem," Tom said. "It gives us a chance to talk business before she gets here."

"Yes, that's true," said Bob. "But, in truth, Tom, I have to ask you... have you made your plans for your heavenly reward? I mean, are you ready for the day when you will meet our Lord and Savior face to face and humble your deeds before his mighty throne?"

Large inquisitive brown eyes stared at Tom above the aviator-framed glasses on the end of Pastor Bob's nose. The man of the cloth brought his fingertips together in a steeple and then brushed mousy brown wisps of thinning hair off his forehead.

A few moments of awkward silence passed as Tom weighed the question. *Is there a wrong answer?*

"Umm... well Bob... Are any of us ready for that day? I mean, meeting your maker, that's heavy stuff. I guess none of us knows how we'll react at the end. I only hope I'll be humble, ask forgiveness and pray my good deeds have outweighed my worldly sins." Tom paused, pleased with his bullshit response.

Pastor Bob stared into Tom's eyes, wanting details, more information.

Tom struggled for a proper bible verse as a trickle of cold sweat ran down his back. Then he remembered something from his catechism. "Bob, what could I possibly offer compared with what our Lord has already sacrificed? 'For God so loved the world, that he gave his only begotten Son, that whosoever believeth in him should not perish, but have everlasting life,' John, 3:16."

"Amen," said a satisfied Pastor Bob.

About to breathe a sigh of relief, Tom's phone began buzzing. He pulled it from his pocket. A text from Lance glared from the screen.

`"Help. Now. Men's room."`

Tom coughed and considered what to do next. "Bob, would you excuse me? I think I'd better head to the restroom myself. Freshen up while we wait for Babs?"

Pastor Bob waved his approval and looked back down at his menu. "Of course, Tom. I'll hold down the fort."

Tom excused himself and hustled back to find Lance.

In the restroom, Tom discovered his partner struggling with not only a lack of intestinal fortitude, but a lack of toilet paper. And the necessary water volume needed to flush his vast offering.

"I need a plunger, dammit!" Lance screamed when Tom entered the men's room. Tom searched, knowing Lance's bathroom habits could create an ark-worthy flood. Then he spied a crusty plunger parked in the corner of the restroom. He brought it to Lance, who stood in the stall doorway, pants around his ankles.

"Jesus H. Christ, Lance! I really wish I didn't just see that."

"Sorry, buddy," Lance said. "Hey, can you see if there's any extra toilet paper around? I mean, since you're here and all."

Tom threw Lance the dirtiest look he could muster, then walked over to the handicapped stall and grabbed the loose roll on top of the holder. He tossed it to Lance, who missed the catch. Tom watched it roll behind the toilet. Lance reached behind him to retrieve it and waved his thanks.

Anxious to get back to the table, Tom barked commands to his partner. "For God's sake, Lance, close the door. And hurry up! I've got to get back out there."

While Lance finished up his business in the bathroom, Tom entertained Pastor Bob, and grew increasingly frustrated. At last, Lance returned armed with an excuse for his lengthy absence. "So, I noticed a deficiency in the bathroom's plumbing system, and I..."

"That's enough, Lance. Pastor Bob was just about to tell me about a retreat he led into the wilderness surrounding the Revelations Retreat Community," said Tom.

"That's right, boys," said Pastor Bob. "I am fortunate enough to have witnessed a true and holy experience on my retreat—in fact, it is altogether worthy of being called an absolute, honest to God almighty miracle."

"Really?" asked Lance, cutting off Pastor Bob. "That's cool. I went on a retreat once. It was when I was still in high school, and my Sunday school class had voted to go to the—"

Tom whipped around and scowled at Lance. "Yes, thank you. Please, Bob. Continue with your story. We'd love to hear all about it."

"Well, like I was saying," Bob continued, "as you boys know, the Revelations Retreat Community Center has had an increase in the numbers of Christians hoping to improve their standing with our Lord prior to the Second Coming. So, we've developed an adventure camp for the God-fearing. You know... get in touch with your inner soul, and discover how to repent after a lifetime of sin and egregious behavior. The group on this particular retreat included some of the most devout members of my church family. They came to prepare for the Second Coming of our Lord. Pastor Bob paused, pushing his glasses up higher on his nose. "And, well, also to hone their survival skills."

"Why, that sounds very interesting, Bob," said Lance. "Like I started saying, when I was—"

"Lance!" barked Tom. "Please stop interrupting Pastor Bob."

Lance crossed his arms and pushed back from the table, sticking out his lower lip in a pout. "I'm sorry, Pastor Bob. Go on."

"Yes, well gentlemen, I took a group of twenty out into the undeveloped part of the ranch. There's not much out there yet, but it's a beautiful spot in the heart of the Blue Ridge Mountains. I haven't cleared the land. After all, that's the point of a biblical retreat, right? So we headed out with our backpacks to see if we could live off the land for ten days. Since this was our first retreat, we weren't sure what we'd find."

Tom started to fidget in his seat, but caught himself. He pulled out his Tiffany pen and drummed it on the table.

Pastor Bob continued droning on in his southern drawl. "Eight women and twelve men all set out to see what the Lord had in store for us. When we set off, I had absolutely no idea where we would end up. You see, I was counting on the Lord to give me direction, boys. I knew he'd divinely intervene and show me the way, just as he always has."

Tom glanced over and caught Lance knuckle-deep into his nose with his pointer finger.

Bob, oblivious to their boredom kept going. "That first day we walked about ten miles, headed straight for nowhere in particular." Pastor Bob chuckled, "Anyway, we decided to set up camp close to one of the streams that passes through the property. That way, we could wash up a bit, and start a fire, boil some drinking water."

At the pause, Tom looked up to see Bob staring at him. He gave a nod, hoping Pastor Bob would wrap up.

"So, once we had the tents set up, and a fire going, we decided we should look for food."

Lance nearly spit up his drink. "You mean, you didn't take any food with you? Nothing?"

Tom kicked his partner under the table, almost hoping Lance would lose interest in the story.

"That's right, no food. Only some utensils, pots, pans—a mess kit each person brought along in their pack. I did bring a big jug to store our water in, once we boiled it. Some wooden spoons for cooking, and a cup, fork, knife, and spoon for each person. I carried those in *my* pack."

Tom restrained a snicker. *Yeah, huge sacrifice, Bob.*

"So anyway, some of the flock got a little down. You know, tired from all the walking. You wouldn't believe what those women wore to walk in. Flip flops—honestly, you'd think they'd have the good sense to bring decent shoes on a journey like this, but—"

"*Jesus,*" Tom interrupted, then realized what he'd said, and added, "was surely with you every step of the way." *Dodged a bullet!* "Did people understand what they were getting into with this? They paid a lot of money for this experience, right? Did they get angry when they found out they had to forage for food?"

"Well, Tom," Pastor Bob answered, "yes and no. Some folks got a might peeved by that. You see, the language in the brochure may have led them to believe food was included in the excursion; however, I knew our Lord would provide... and boys, he did."

"Do tell," Tom blurted, but then flashed a charming smile to try to cover up the sarcasm. He decided it might be better just to let his mind wander.

Tom had heard about Pastor Bob's adventure camps, and how he scammed gullible parishioners out of their hard earned tithes. If Pastor Bob's followers benefitted from these excursions, then more power to him. But he had heard disturbing rumors about the overnight couples' retreats, called, "Erotica as God intended: Create your own Garden of Eden."

Tom found the concept appalling. Pastor Bob had suggested he and Vicky might want to come and check out the program. *"If you are looking for a more harmonious coupling with the Lord's blessing..."* Tom cringed at the memory.

Conveniently located near several major interstates, all of these adventure camps took place at a pricey lodge not far from the church's headquarters.

"Boys, things improved a tad when we had the water situation under control. It calmed down the people who were looking for flush toilets. I dug the latrine pit myself. Since no one volunteered."

Lance shot Pastor Bob an enthusiastic thumbs up for support.

"I decided everyone should spend some time in quiet meditation and reflect on how our Lord survived forty days in the desert, while I did some serious soul searching and praying. I hoped with all my heart, that the Lord would give me some direction, as he always has. I hoped he'd show me how to care for this flock of lost sheep, all looking for guidance, and enlightenment."

Lance yawned loudly and then blew his nose with a crusty handkerchief pulled from his pocket.

Tom glared daggers at his associate, then forced himself to make intentional eye contact with Bob to show at least one of them was still interested.

Pastor Bob cleared his throat and continued, "After three hours of meditating and praying, I was getting a little concerned. Then all of a sudden, I heard a loud flap of wings, and a great squawking. I opened my eyes and blinked a couple of times to make sure I wasn't seeing things. But sure enough, right there down by the creek was a flock of wild turkeys. In fact, five of the biggest turkeys I've ever seen in my life.

"I got up, quiet as I could, and made my way to the stream. I got closer and closer to the turkeys, but they didn't budge. In fact, one of those magnificent birds left the group, and started walking toward me."

Tom's eyebrows rose up in disbelief.

"Do you know I stopped walking and stood as still as a statue, waiting to see what that turkey was up to, not sure what I should do next? Then, as it got within about two feet from where I stood, it occurred to me this was the answer to my prayers. God was telling me to reach out and wring that poor turkey's neck. And boys, that's exactly what I did."

Tom's hand rose up to his throat as he stifled a gasp.

A server approached with drinks and the appetizers, and delivered a written message saying Babs wouldn't be joining them after all. Pastor Bob excused himself to phone his wife for details, freeing Lance to interrogate the server about the dinner specials. He questioned methods of preparation, the cleanliness of the kitchen and the formal training of the chef and other kitchen personnel. As usual, he ordered something not on the regular menu—steak tartare.

Pastor Bob finished his phone call and ordered the filet of sole. Tom, horrified by Lance's behavior, ordered another glass of wine and the veal marsala.

Despite the commotion, Tom noticed a ruckus at the neighboring table, where the little boy had been playing. A loud scream pierced the air and the parents stood over their hysterical child. A member of the management staff rushed over to investigate, while the boy's mother pointed to her child's head and screamed.

Although sympathetic, Tom couldn't help craning his neck for a better view. He saw what was dangling from the boy's head. *The mousetrap!* Complete with dead mouse, the mousetrap was now attached to the little boy's curly blond hair.

The manager held up a large red napkin from the table to shield the boy from other curious diners, and whisked the distraught family away.

Unmoved by the crying youngster, Lance barely looked up from the table. "I'll never understand why people try to take little kids to a nice restaurant like this. It never works out."

"Truly spoken, brother," answered Pastor Bob. "Spare the rod, spoil the child I always say!"

"Excuse me, please," said Tom. "I need to find the restroom. Again."

"Watch out for stall number two," called Lance.

Tom turned and glared again at Lance who merely shrugged. Then he headed to the men's room, where he washed his hands, splashed some water on his face and stared at his reflection. He needed to calm down before he went back out there. He tried to take some deep breaths, but the air in the restroom smelled like dirty diapers and industrial strength cleaning products.

Forcing himself to concentrate on deep even breaths, he willed himself to relax. He couldn't have a panic attack in front of a client. Tom reached into his pocket and took a small white pill from the tiny vial, and dry swallowed the tablet. Within a few minutes, his pulse slowed down and his anxiety lessened.

He headed back out to the table, and as soon as he sat down, Pastor Bob said, "Oh, good you're back. Couldn't finish my testament without you here." Pastor Bob looked at Tom and winked. "I'm telling you boys it was a miracle. Every day, the Lord our God blessed us with a sacrificial turkey."

So the story went, for the rest of the retreat, a wild turkey appeared—only to Pastor Bob, of course—and without any other witnesses present. Day after day, the faithful gathered, and waited for the turkey to appear, to no avail. Finally, bored and disinterested, the group left and went to look for berries. And each day, just when the group thought their lucky streak had ended, Pastor Bob returned with another miracle turkey in hand—its neck neatly wrung, gutted, and ready to be plucked.

Bob admitted the retreat proved more difficult than he had imagined. Without the daily arrival of the sacrificial turkey, it would have been far worse, but needless to say, by the end of the adventure, Pastor Bob and his flock were ready to return home. Their spiritual retreat proved prolific though. The adventure provided inspiration for many sermons in the weeks and months to come in the church; in fact, it was through his sermons and reliving the adventures of the wild turkey divination that the media got wind of the story. The parable became legendary in Pastor Bob's church, and he was pleased to note—without a trace of bragging—that his membership had increased dramatically since the story was featured on the local news station, WSOB.

Tom struggled to say something, but could only muster a dry cough. Luckily, the waitress arrived with their entrees nixing the need for insincere flattery.

"Pastor Bob," Lance said, leaning in with his tie dangling precariously close to the pile of what looked like raw hamburger on his plate, "what an amazing story. It's hard to believe something like that could happen in this day and age."

"Lance, that's enough," Tom chided. "I'm sure Pastor Bob doesn't need to hear any of this."

"It's okay, son. I had my share of doubters and naysayers interrogating me during that television interview. Folks accused me of planting turkeys! Can you imagine that? I mean, we were out in the middle of nowhere. It's not like I had the Winn Dixie making deliveries every day."

Tom rolled his eyes and said nothing. He tried to forget about plungers, sticky mousetraps, traumatized young families and Pastor Bob's newfound status as a sacrificial turkey celebrity. He sighed and cut into his veal.

CHAPTER EIGHT

Tom stretched out his long legs beneath his desk, and stared out the office window. He seldom daydreamed, but today his responsibilities weighed him down like stones in the pocket of a drowning man. The computer screen on his desk hummed and buzzed with the daily rollercoaster of the stock exchange. Beeping, flashing graphs charted today's speculation and left him hypnotized.

The ringing of his cell snapped him out of trance. He glanced down to see Doyle was calling and picked up on the third ring.

"Yo! Freaking FRYE MAN! What's up, b-r-o-t-h-e-r?" Doyle dragged out the last word in every greeting.

Tom pulled the phone away from his ear and winced. "Jesus, Doyle. Do you always have to fucking scream? It's early, man."

"HAHAHAHA! Pussy! What's wrong with you, man? Did I wake you up?"

"No. I'm in the office, getting ready to head out for Economics Club. What's up with you?"

"Listen dude, I wanted to give you a heads up. I'm like 99 percent sure that Santa Sam is gonna ditch his hottie wife."

"What? Where'd you hear that? I'm supposed to see them later this morning."

"Yeah, man. I know that. The Santa Man called me yesterday and hinted around. Asked me to clarify a few things in his pre-nup with Rita. That's always a bad sign. At least, historically speaking. Usually he double checks this shit with me *before* he ditches the wife *du jour*."

"Hmmm. No shit. Well, it's news to me," said Tom. "I haven't heard anything."

"So, yeah, I think he's gonna spring it on everyone today at your meeting. That's my guess. I just wanted you to be prepared for some fireworks to go down."

"All right, I appreciate that. What are you up to today? You in court?"

"Nah. I'm at the golf course, buddy. Too fucking nice out not to squeeze in nine holes. Okay, chief. I'm up. Gotta run. Good luck."

"Yeah—" Tom heard a click in his ear before he even finished. "Well, shit."

He looked at his calendar. Booked solid with an Economics Club meeting at 7:00 A.M., followed by the meeting with Sam Boogher and his wife Rita. Sam, now sixty-five, had made a fortune in automobile salvage, and for the last twenty years Tom had been at his beck and call. Sam had dubbed himself "Sexy Santa," embracing his enormous belly, white hair and full beard. Somehow he managed to land Rita, his stunning and much younger fourth wife.

Getting involved in another Boogher divorce made Tom nervous. "Hmmm. This could be a real shit storm," he said aloud.

Santa Sam had many weaknesses and used his staggering wealth to indulge without apologies. Weakness number one: the ladies. Weakness number two: Patrón silver tequila. And weakness number three was having no self-control when combining numbers one and two, which happened frequently.

After Economics Club, Tom prepped for the Boogher meeting. It was still early, so he studied the financial data streaming across the bottom of his computer screen. He gathered the forms and prospectuses he needed to wrap up his other appointments this week and checked the *Wall Street* headlines.

Clients questioned him about financial trends, and he needed to take care he didn't miss something they might read about or see on the evening news. Most of all they worried a drastic correction in the market was imminent, but he wasn't so sure. The faint of heart who had bailed out after the 2008 crash still hadn't recovered psychologically, and they probably never would.

A text from Vicky interrupted his train of thought.

`Dates? Don't forget. You promised.`

Vicky's text was punctuated by the smiling, winking, kissy-face emoji.

`Okay. Working on it.`

He had promised Vicky he would get things cleaned up enough to take a few days off, and he wanted to keep his word. He perused the shared staff calendar and had just found some possible dates for their mini-vacation, when Peggy buzzed on the intercom. "Tom, Rita Boogher is on line one for you. She says it's urgent."

"Thanks. Put her through."

Great. Probably running late again.

After a brief pause, Tom heard Rita crying. "Tom, I need you to come out to the house. We aren't going to be able to come into your office today." Rita sniffed loudly in his ear.

"Yeah, sure, Rita. What's going on?"

Rita explained she had come home from the gym and found the locks changed. Most of her clothes were strewn across the front lawn. Several large suitcases, stuffed to capacity, had been tossed into the arborvitae. Rita had only planned to stop at home long enough to change clothes, but she was shocked at what she found.

"Tom, I don't know what to do. Sam and I talked about all this last night. He knew I was going to the gym this morning, like I always do. He suggested we drive separately to meet at your office, though. I thought it was strange, but you know Sam."

Now he won't answer the door. Can you come over? I know he'll come out if you're here."

"Sure, Rita. I'll be right over. See you in thirty minutes."

Tom hung up and gathered the documents he needed for their meeting.

Could it be Sam has wife number five lined up?

Tom knew they had an odd marriage, and they fought a lot. No doubt Sam used jewelry and expensive trips to pacify his wife. Still, Sam had a violent temper, and he'd known Rita to burst into tears at the slightest provocation.

God, I hate it when women cry during these meetings.

He stopped in front of Peggy's desk. "Change in plans. I'm going to the Boogher's instead. There's something going on over there I need to check out."

"All right. But is the meeting with Don Graybill happening this week? You never told me if they scheduled it. I need to know if I'm going along to notarize, you know?"

Tom stared and said nothing.

"I have a life too, Tom. A family. Responsibilities..."

Peggy, always the smartass. Tom smacked his forehead. "Oh, right. I never heard back. Could you call Graybill's secretary? Thanks."

He darted away before Peggy could argue with him. Out of the corner of his eye he saw her glaring as she picked up the phone. He knew she hated making follow-up calls.

Tom arrived at the Boogher's upscale, gated community about twenty minutes later and was waved in by the security guard.

As he drove up to the white stone mansion, he witnessed the chaos. After parking he walked toward Rita, who stood on the lawn staring at her things. A mirror laid cracked on the driveway, small pieces of glass shimmering in the sun. Purses, scarves, bags, and shoes by the dozen scattered the property like remnants from a garage sale. Bras, underwear, and toiletries tumbled everywhere.

She motioned for him to join her. "Okay, Tom. Watch this."

She marched to the front door and entered her access code again. No luck. The home alarm system blared as lights flashed and sirens cut through the humid air. Rita rang the doorbell and pounded on the door with her fists. Tom put his hands over his ears to muffle the noise.

The door opened, showing a sliver of the pretty maid's face. "Hola, Señora."

"Stand aside and let me come in," said Rita.

"Lo siento, Señora, but Señor Santa does not wish you to come in," said the maid.

"What? What the hell is going on?" Rita screamed. "You let me in right this minute. I have Mr. Frye with me. Go tell Señor Santa Mr. Frye is here. He'll come out."

But the maid didn't budge.

Rita lunged and forced her to the side of the doorway, but a large, age-spotted, hairy hand appeared and grabbed her from the other side of the door. Sam had hidden there all along, listening like the coward he was.

"Hold it right there, sweetheart. You're not getting any further," said Sam.

"What are you doing? Why are you doing this to me? I don't understand." Rita continued trying to force through the doorway but Sam grabbed ahold of her arm and kept her at the threshold.

Tom stepped forward to interject.

"What are you doing here, Tom?" Sam paused to look at the large watch on his wrist. "Our meeting's not for another forty minutes. We'll be there. Now, if you'll excuse me, I've got some housekeeping to take care of. Time for you to go, Tom."

Sam took a step toward Tom, still holding onto Rita's wrist. Tom took two steps back, his eyes pinned on the struggling couple.

"All right, I just want to make sure everybody's calmed down, and then I'll go. But—"

The blare of sirens interrupted him. Tom watched as the police, a fire truck, and an ambulance pulled into the driveway.

Sam released Rita's wrist and pushed her out the door and onto the front porch. He moved toward the responders, and addressed the burly police officer in the lead. "Hey guys, thanks for coming so quickly. I apologize—there's no emergency, just a little misunderstanding between my wife and me."

"Officer. He's lost his mind," Rita yelled. "He's locked me out of the house, and thrown my clothes all over the yard. Please, do something!"

Tom watched as the cop cocked an eyebrow in surprise.

Probably wonders how a paunchy old man got lucky enough to land this hot little brunette.

Sam wore torn dirty old blue jeans, littered with food stains, and a red and black plaid flannel shirt circa 1970. His enormous potbelly loomed over a cracked leather belt, and his long white hair tangled into his crusty beard.

Jesus, he looks like a homeless Santa Claus.

The cop locked eyes with Tom, who smiled, shrugged his shoulders and opened his mouth to speak.

But Sam interrupted again. "Pay no attention to the guy in the suit," he said, hooking a thumb in Tom's direction. "He's just leaving, aren't you, Tom?"

Everyone turned to Tom for clarification.

"Ah, yes. I'm leaving. I'll see you both at the appointment." Tom looked at Rita, pointed to his watch and mouthed 'see you soon.' She nodded and wiped her nose with her hand again.

Tom jumped into his car, and craned his neck to watch the drama unfold. The cop stood between the couple with his arms folded and nodded occasionally. Sam reached into his back pocket and handed something to the officer.

A restraining order? Divorce papers?

Tom was dying of curiosity, but he started the car and drove past them with his window open. He pulled over and parked along the curb, just within earshot, and pretended to rummage through his briefcase for something.

Sam whipped his head around and gave Tom a dirty look. His bushy eyebrows knitted together, but then he turned back to his conversation.

Whatever. I need to know what the fuck is going on here.

Even with his window and sunroof open and no radio, he could barely hear the conversation.

"Ma'am, I'm afraid your husband has taken out a restraining order against you," said the officer. "He's claiming he fears for his life. It states you need to stay at least 100 feet away from him at all times, and you're not to set foot on the property—of which he is the sole owner."

The cop, who looked old enough to be a seasoned veteran of the force, continued. "I think he intends to keep you out of the house permanently. To make room for his 'new future wife.' His words, ma'am, not mine. Sorry." He looked at Rita, who continued to sob.

"New wife? What new wife? Jesus, Sam, we haven't even been married for five years yet!"

"Now, Rita. Calm down. I told you a long time ago I never keep a wife past the age of forty. You're forty-two. I kept you around a couple of extra years. Just to be nice. I kinda felt sorry for you. Until now, that is."

"What? You never told me any such thing."

"Double check the pre-nup sweetie, I believe you'll find it in there somewhere."

"You can't do this to me. That's ridiculous. You're making that up."

"Nope. Double check. I believe it's on page seven, paragraph eleven."

Sam reached into his back pants pocket and produced another document. He pulled his glasses from the pocket of his shirt, flipped through the pages and scanned. A few seconds later he pointed his big finger at a segment on the page and thrust the paper at Rita.

She looked too stunned to react.

"You should always read what you sign, sweetheart."

"Look," said the officer, "I really don't know what the hell's going on here, but I'll tell you this. Expect a bill from Emergency Services for this little charade." The officer tipped his hat to Rita, who was crying even harder now. "Ma'am. Good luck to you." He turned to the responders hanging around. "Okay, guys, let's get out of here. Just another domestic dispute." The fire fighters and ambulance crew climbed into their vehicles and drove off.

Tom started his car and pulled away behind the cop car. He had plenty of shit to sort through before the meeting later this morning.

God. This will be a circus.

As he drove back to his office, Tom wondered why Sam insisted they keep today's appointment. He hadn't been happy to see him at the house. Tom tried to ignore a gnawing sense of dread. Sam had no sense of loyalty. He used people and tossed them aside like dirty Kleenex. Was Sam about to get rid of him as well?

On the walk to his office Tom's chest grew tight and his pulse quickened. He needed to stay calm. He closed his eyes, leaned against the door and fought the mounting anxiety. Deep breaths didn't calm him. He reached into his pocket for the vial. Just one. He needed it today.

Tom had already been through this drill with Santa Sam before. Twice. And Rita was two years past her expiration date. When it came to Santa Sam and his wives, it was useless. Santa Sam liked his women young, buxom and under forty; and he took romantic advice from no one. His penis overruled his brain.

Back at the office, Tom had calmed down a bit when he heard shouting coming from the reception area. He sat at his desk and listened.

Is that Lance and Peggy making such a racket?

When he couldn't stand it any longer, he went out to see what was going on. Rita sat crying at Peggy's desk, and Santa Sam stood alone by the elevator. Sam, reading glasses perched on the end of his nose, stared at his Blackberry. When he spotted Tom, he yawned and walked over.

"Hey, Sam," Tom greeted, not quite knowing what to say.

"Oh, so you're here after all," Sam replied. "Well, good. You take care of Rita, all right? Get her set up with whatever she needs to move on. Double check the email I shot off to you this morning with all my stipulations. There's nothing out of the ordinary, just a few things to clarify before she moves out." He turned and looked at his wife. "Rita, hold yourself together. You knew this was coming, after all."

"Email?" said Tom. "I haven't had a chance to—"

Rita jumped up and shook her fist at Sam. "Just get out, you bastard! I hate you, you dirty old man! I can't believe you're doing this to me. All of the bullshit I've put up with—erectile dysfunction, sauerkraut colonics, your spiritual shaman. You make me sick. You're insane. Just get out of here and leave me alone."

Tom steered Sam to the elevator, and pushed the down button. Thank God no one else was in the waiting room. "I'll call you after I review the email," Tom said.

"Whaddaya mean, 'after you review it'? You didn't read it yet?" said Sam.

"No. I had an early breakfast meeting with the Economics Club, then I went out to *your* house, and I just got back to the office. I haven't had a chance to check email yet. I'll look everything over and give you a call ASAP."

Sam stepped into the elevator. "Ya know what? You're fired. Don't bother doing anything. You'll be hearing from my attorneys. Nice knowin' ya."

Tom pushed his hand against the elevator door to keep it open. "Sam, you're upset. Let's not be hasty. I'll call you. We'll figure things out."

"After what I saw today—" He stopped and looked Tom in the eye. "You'll hear something, one way or another. No promises."

The elevator door closed. Tom took a long deep breath and turned around to face Rita. "Come in my office so we can talk."

Tom hated to tell Rita he couldn't do much to help her. As much as he liked her, Santa Sam was the guy with the cash. He had to make amends with Sam. No matter the cost to his ego.

Rita started screaming as soon as she sat down. "Do you know that son of a bitch actually cut off my credit cards? How can he do that? Just make a phone call and pull the plug? How am I supposed to survive?"

Rita's big blue eyes were swimming with tears again, and Tom cringed. After years of dealing with psychotic secretaries, teenaged daughters and a pre-menopausal wife, he was exhausted. Crying women made him anxious and angry.

"Well, Rita, it is unfair. I'm the first one to agree with you about that. But I think instead of focusing on the negative here—and I'm sure that is easier said than done—let's try and come up with some ideas for you to—" Tom struggled to find the right words, "rebuild."

He tried to smile. Once upon a time he would have been more compassionate, but he was tired of working with clients who couldn't stay married. He hated picking sides.

"Rebuild? How do I do that? I've been locked out of my house, and my bank account. I've had my clothes thrown across what used to be my front yard. He cut off my credit cards, and ended our marriage by handing me an envelope with fifty thousand dollars in cash. If I didn't have my dog to keep me company in bed, I'd be sleeping alone, too." More angry tears spilled down her face and splashed onto the desktop.

Again, Tom found himself without a box of tissues. Another reason to be annoyed by crying. *Dammit.*

He picked up the phone and paged his secretary. "Peggy, can you please bring a box of tissues in here?"

"What for?" Peggy asked. "Where am I supposed to find tissues? I don't have any here. I guess I could ask around—"

"For God's sake, just get in here. Now!" Tom slammed the phone and whispered to Rita. "Sorry."

Peggy tromped into the office. "What?"

Tom reached into his wallet and threw a twenty-dollar bill at her. "Go buy some tissues. Please."

"Okay," Peggy said. She hesitated. "How many boxes should I buy?"

"As many as you can get for twenty bucks."

"Well, which store should I go to? I mean, I could drive over to BJ's, but that'd take a while. Or I could go to Giant, or I guess I could look online to see if there are any coupons—"

"Just go to Rite Aid, across the street, Peggy. I'm sure they have tissues there."

Peggy stared for a moment, then looked at her watch. "Well, it's almost lunchtime, if I could just wait about an hour, then I could—"

"Now, Peggy. Go now. I need the tissues now."

"Okay. Well, is there a particular brand you want? Because, I mean, I could pick up something, you know, like, nice, or do you want the bargain brand? Personally, I like Puffs because they're so soft, and—"

"Buy whatever you want. But I need them now. Hurry. Please."

"Okay, I'm going. I'm going," Peggy said. "I was just trying to be nice. I guess I shouldn't ask about the 'rewards card', right?"

Tom rolled his eyes in response.

Peggy slinked off, but paused again before she got to the door. She opened her mouth to say something else but then changed her mind. Another eye roll from her boss, and she left for the store.

Embarrassed by this mini *coup d'état*, Tom rummaged around in his desk. He might have a roll of toilet paper from the last time this happened. Dammit all. He found the smashed but still usable roll and handed it across to Rita.

She sniffed and coughed in between tears. "Thanks."

"Okay now, let's get back to talking about finding some help for you," Tom said. "First, do you have an attorney? If not I can give you a couple of recommendations. Tell them I referred you."

Rita nodded, unable to speak.

Tom fished several cards from his desk drawer and handed them to her. "Now, I can refer you to someone in the bank who can get you set up with an account—just for you—that way you can get checks, a card, all that jazz, so you feel normal again."

"What do you mean 'refer me', Tom? You can't do that for me?"

Uh oh. Here it goes.

"Well, as much as I'd like to, I'm afraid I can't. I've worked with Sam for twenty years, and I can't get caught in the middle of your divorce. Unfortunately, the bank has restrictions prohibiting me from keeping you as a client. You see—"

"Oh, I get it," Rita interrupted. "You can't change teams. Is that it? Or, oh no, wait! I don't make enough money to be one of your clients. Right? Well, that's great."

"Now Rita, please don't make it sound that way. I'm sorry, I am, but I wouldn't be able to give you the attention you need right now."

He rummaged through his desk drawer and pulled out another stack of referral cards. He thumbed through it and handed one over. "Here you go. Call this woman. She's great. You'll love her. In fact, she took my old job in Private Banking at Mellon."

Rita snatched the card and stood up. "Well, thanks for nothing. I'd better shove off if I need to reinvent my entire life by the end of the day." She turned and threw the roll of toilet paper at his head. It caught him in the temple. "Oops, sorry about that. By the way, does your banker friend rent apartments too? I still need to find a place for me and my poodle to live."

She stormed out of the office with Tom close behind. On her way to the elevator, she ran into Peggy who was carrying a plastic bag.

"Leaving already?" asked Peggy. "Well, let us know if you need anything else."

Reaching over, Rita snatched a box of Puffs Plus from the top of Peggy's shopping bag. "Thanks. This'll do." Sniffing, she took a long last look at Peggy and Tom and climbed into the elevator with her box of tissues.

CHAPTER NINE

Tom gritted his teeth as he drove to his 8:00 A.M. dentist appointment. He hated the x-rays most of all. Those massive metal contraptions made his gag reflex spring into action. It embarrassed and annoyed him. He hadn't had an x-ray in over three years, but he'd broken his tooth eating those damn Swedish Fish. Thanks again, Mina Stab.

He forced himself to think about scheduling his upcoming meeting with Don Graybill, the CEO of a large furniture manufacturing company. The meeting needed to happen soon, but scheduling anything with Graybill was next to impossible. Graybill, an elusive man, had scores of minions to do all of his dirty work for him. Multiple accountants, attorneys, and personal assistants looked after him. Even the personal assistants had personal assistants. One thing was certain. All meetings were scheduled at the convenience of Mr. Graybill. *They* would contact *you* when it suited. Considering the guy got started right after college making furniture in his parents' garage, he had done very well.

Graybill had been a client for over a dozen years, but Tom had never met him in person. The minions handled whatever came up, and Tom never saw the guy face to face. But now, the mystery man needed to refinance one of his private planes. This supposed corporate jet was one of Mr. Graybill's expensive but necessary playthings, and had a price tag of ten million dollars.

A typical refinancing was pesky, but not difficult. However, this situation was complicated. The bank needed to file a lien for the plane in Tulsa, Oklahoma, where the FAA had a hub; and this deal required approval from the FAA itself, which meant scores of documents needed Graybill's signature. All of this minimized the chance of fraudulent activity.

So, Tom passed the information along to the attorneys and others in the corporate food chain. He needed to personally witness Don Graybill signing these documents—in the presence of a notary public. He needed to meet with Graybill and his underlings face to face.

He decided to call the head of Graybill's legal team, Attorney Fred Kline, while en route to the dentist. Maybe Kline had an idea when they could wrap up this deal. After the two exchanged pleasantries, the tone turned ugly.

"What do you mean, you need to witness his signature?" Kline asked. "He's an extremely busy man, Tom. You can't expect him to do that. The man has millions of dollars in your bank. Can't some exceptions be made? He's a very private guy."

"Fred, I wish I could, believe me. But we're talking about ten million dollars, coupled with multitudes of FAA regulations and a bank I've never heard of somewhere in Oklahoma."

Tom paused, and waited for a reaction on the other end of the phone. He continued, "Listen, I plan on making this as painless for your boss as possible. I'll be at your disposal day or night. Call when it suits you, and I'll bring the documents over for his signature. My assistant is a notary. I'll bring her with me so we can get this wrapped up." A long silence punctuated the conversation.

"Tom, I don't have to tell you, this is highly irregular—I mean—unheard of. Really. For a man of his stature in the community to have to jump through these kinds of hoops, it's ridiculous. But it sounds like we have no choice."

Kline sighed and paused for a moment.

"I dread telling him this, Tom. He's not going to be happy. I'm not even sure he's in the damn country. Last I heard he was in Myanmar. And I hope this won't make him rethink who he does business with in this town."

Tom cleared his throat. "Just let me know when he'll be around, Fred. I'll have all the documents ready to go. Keep in touch, right?"

The phone clicked loudly in his ear, followed by the dial tone—a familiar theme, of late. *Well, that was fun.*

Tom arrived at the dentist and headed to check in with the receptionist. An elderly woman with large eyeglasses opened the sliding glass window and crossed his name off the list as soon as he signed in.

"They'll be with you shortly, hon," she said and slid the glass window shut.

Tom took a seat and pretended to browse through a magazine while he waited for his time in the chair. He tried to remain calm, but he had that anxious, jittery feeling fluttering in his stomach. He took some deep breaths, trying to breathe in through the nose, and out through the mouth. *Damn it, I should've taken a pill.*

He heard his name called. *Shit, it's time!*

An attractive young woman approached him, "Come on back, Mr. Frye. How're you doing this morning?"

"Fabulous," Tom said, but his sarcasm appeared lost on the hygienist.

"Have a seat and let's take a look at your chart, shall we?" She flipped on the computer screen and studied the pictures. "Mr. Frye, it looks like you're past due for x-rays? Looks like it's been oh, about five years since you let us take any pictures. What's the matter, are you camera shy?" The hygienist laughed, an annoying nasal sort of laugh that grated on his nerves.

"Nope, no fight today. Do your worst," Tom said.

"Really? Awesome. Hold on, I'll be right back." She fastened the disposable dental bib around Tom's neck and started digging through the instruments at her station. "Okay, well, here it is. This is what I need," she said.

Tom heard more banging and clanging and watched the girl carry over a tray of hopefully sterilized x-ray tools.

"Okay, let's get these x-rays out of the way first," she said. She unwrapped the instruments from their sterile wrappers.

Jesus, they look even bigger than I remember.

"Let's open real wide now, Mr. Frye, so we can see what's going on in there."

She moved toward Tom with the large metal device. At once, he felt his stomach lurch. He sat up very straight against the back of the chair, and scooted back as far as he could.

"You okay, Mr. Frye? You look like you've seen a ghost."

"It's just that—that thing is enormous."

"Now there, open wide. We'll be done before you know it."

The hygienist leaned in closer, and pulled Tom's lips back tight against his face. His mouth stretched and contorted as the hygienist struggled to insert the instrument.

"A little wider, oh, that's great. Okay, now hold that position and bite down so I can get the first picture." She walked out of the room and pressed the switch on the wall outside the door. A buzz blasted the room.

When she shut off the x-ray switch, Tom heard a commotion erupting from the reception area. Loud muffled voices drifted into the room, and he could hear doors opening and closing in the hallway.

"What in the world is going on?" the hygienist asked. "Don't move, Mr. Frye. I'll be right back." Tom sat trapped with the dental monstrosity stuck in his mouth.

By now, his gag reflex charged full speed ahead. *What should I do? I'm gonna hurl all over the place. This thing is strangling me. I'm choking! My God! How do I get this out of my mouth?*

He made small guttural noises, miniature muffled screams because his mouth was jammed full of x-ray gear.

More noise and commotion came from the hallway. He looked toward the doorway and saw Peggy forcing her way into the exam room. The brave hygienist protected her turf and blocked the entrance. Tom, who continued to gag, reached up and pulled the device out of his mouth.

"Jesus Christ!" he said. "What the hell is going on? You just left me stranded, with this thing in my mouth. How could you? And Peggy? What are you doing here?"

"Tom, I'm sorry to interrupt, but we need to take those documents over to our... *special* client for signature. You know, the one who's so hard to see? The one we've been waiting to see for two weeks? Tom?" Peggy stopped talking and stared at Tom, dramatic as always.

It took him a minute, but he realized she meant Graybill. *Son of a bitch.*

"We're in the middle of doing Mr. Frye's x-rays," the hygienist said. "You can't just barge in here and pull him out of the chair."

"Honey, I can and I will," said Peggy, "and if you're smart, you'll help me get him out of this getup. We have twenty minutes to get across town in rush hour traffic."

The room buzzed with voices. The receptionist and Dr. Maurice Kirby, D.D.S., now crammed into the exam room with Tom, Peggy, and the hygienist. Everyone talked at once.

Dr. Kirby put his fingers to his mouth and whistled. Silence followed. "What in God's name is going on here, people?" he asked. Dr. Kirby looked like a character from a science-fiction movie with his yellow goggles and full protection body suit. "Oh hey, Tom," he said, snapping off his purple disposable gloves and reaching out to shake hands. "Everything okay here?"

"Hey, Maurice!" said Tom. "I have a client emergency I need to take care of. Can I reschedule my appointment for another day? I'm sorry, but my secretary had strict orders to track me down." Tom looked embarrassed but smiled.

He ripped off the bib, laid it on the tray and looked for the switch to lower the chair. The chair careened up and down until he finally figured out how to lower it. He then grabbed Peggy by the wrist and ran out before the stunned dentist or his staff could say a word.

"Bye, and thanks. I'll call to reschedule," he called as he ran down the hallway, dragging Peggy behind him.

"Well, that was awkward," she said.

"You're coming with me, right?" Tom asked as they made their way across the parking lot. "How much time do we have to get there?"

Peggy tapped her foot as she waited for Tom to unlock the Mercedes. "Not like I have any choice. Besides, we were late twenty minutes ago. I stopped at Starbucks on my way over here. I had such a headache. Needed some caffeine."

Tom sighed, peeled out of the parking lot, and drove like a maniac all the way across town. When they approached the parking lot of the facility, he felt his gut clench. *Oh shit. Not now.* He parked the car in the back of the lot as far away from the guard shack as possible.

He opened the car door and wretched, heaving in the grass until there was nothing left. He glanced around, afraid someone had seen him, but the guard at the gate was busy talking on the phone. When he felt able to walk, he wiped his sweaty face with this handkerchief and popped a Tic Tac in his mouth.

"Okay. I'm ready to go now," he said. He still felt shaky, but they were already running late.

Peggy wrinkled her nose in disgust. "Well, finally. Jeez Louise. Are you sick or something? Gross."

This was going to be one hell of a day. He felt it in his bones.

CHAPTER TEN

Tom had hit a new low. After all, people who had worked for Don Graybill for years had never met him. But yanked out of the dentist's chair to meet Graybill? Not to mention listening to Peggy's incessant chatter on the drive, and now hurling in the bushes? Talk about bad timing.

He understood clients expected flexibility and exemption from regular rules, but the bank refused to negotiate. He honored his client's requests when he could, made exceptions and bent the rules, but corporate banking limited his power.

People like Graybill ignored rules, and wanted bankers who did too. This was where the smaller banks could come in and steal clients. They lurked on the fringe, listened to the business hum in the wind, and hunted clients like vultures for carrion.

When Tom had composed himself enough to drive up to the gate, the security guard waved them into a visitor's spot. They walked into the main building and looked for the receptionist. Still dazed and anxious, he scanned the area and tried to calm himself. *God, this is a big building.*

A sharp stab of pain jolted him. Peggy had elbowed him in the arm. "Ow! What the hell is your problem?"

"You're not paying attention to anything I'm saying. How else am I supposed to get your attention, your majesty? Jeez Louise, some people are cranky today!"

"Cranky? You pulled me out of the damn dentist's chair—literally. Why shouldn't I be cranky? Just shut up. I need to get through this."

"Well, excuse me for living. Oh. There's the receptionist."

They walked through a door into a lavish lobby with plush draperies and comfy leather seating and made their way to the receptionist's window. A pretty brunette smiled and slid the glass open to greet them.

"May I help you?"

"Good morning. Tom Frye. Mr. Graybill is expecting me?" He tried to smile again. Then he whirled around, and sweetened his tone. He had acted badly this morning, even though Peggy deserved it. "You have all of your stuff, right? Your notary seal, the documents, everything we need?"

"Got it all right here. I have to admit I'm kinda excited to meet *the* Don Graybill!" Peggy gushed. "He's like a legend in this town."

Tom straightened his tie and flicked imaginary dust from his suit coat.

"Yes sir, Mr. Frye," said the receptionist. "I'll let them know you're here. Could you have a seat over there and make yourselves comfortable? Someone should be out shortly to bring you back."

"Thanks for introducing me, too," sniped Peggy as they sat down. "You know, you really don't respect me at all. It's very insulting."

"Sorry," he said. "I'll make it up to you." He sat down and ignored her while she continued to glare. Tom glanced at his watch: 9:35. *Only five minutes late. That's not too bad. Jesus, considering the short notice, it's a miracle we're here at all. Just keep calm.*

Fifteen minutes later, they were still waiting. Tom's anxiety continued to rise. He tapped his foot and cracked his knuckles. He stared at the crossword puzzle in the *People* magazine. He wasn't up on celebrities, but the photo in the center square of the puzzle was of Hillary Clinton. Hah! She wasn't a celebrity. He pulled out his pen and added a full beard, moustache and devil horns to the photo. He felt a little better.

Annoyed, Peggy reached over and grabbed the pen out of his hand. "Settle down!" she whispered. "Honestly, you're making *me* nervous!"

"Sorry. I hate waiting."

A few moments later, he glanced up as a small, very compact-looking man made his way toward them. Tom did a double take, thinking at first it was Danny DeVito, the actor. But it wasn't. *Stupid magazine has me imagining celebrities.*

The tiny man approached and reached out to shake hands. "Mr. Frye? Alan Drysdale, chief financial officer. Good to meet you. And who might this lovely young lady be with you?" He winked at Peggy, who pushed in front of Tom to say hello.

"Oh, this is Peggy, my executive assistant. She's here to notarize the forms Mr. Graybill is signing today."

"The more the merrier," said Drysdale. "Please follow me." His stubby little arms pointed in the direction of double-bolted doors where he stopped and punched in a long security code on the keypad. They passed through several long straight hallways secured by steel doors and security codes. Every twenty or thirty feet, another doorway and another access code to punch in.

Peggy walked next to Drysdale and made random comments about the level of security.

"This reminds me of that old television show *Get Smart*," she said. "Remember that show, Tom? With Agent 99 and Max and the Chief. I was crazy about it when I was a kid. Cracked me up."

Tom shot his secretary a stern look and made swift motions between his head and neck—the universal sign for 'cut it out.'

Drysdale appeared amused. But Tom had to admit that Peggy had hit on something. Why did a manufacturing plant—of wooden furniture no less—go to such extremes to protect their turf?

What could be so top secret about making furniture? Okay, it's handcrafted, made in the USA, claimed lumbar support and the wood was from a rainforest somewhere in

South America. But it's furniture. Blasted Peggy! Distracting me again.

He needed complete control and focus when he met Graybill. Out of the corner of his eye, he watched as Peggy continued talking a blue streak. Tom walked faster to catch up.

"Mr. Drysdale," Peggy crooned. "I'm sure you hear this all the time, but has anyone ever told you, you look like Danny Devito? I just love him. He's so talented! Remember that movie with Bette Midler? What was it called? Oh, *Ruthless People*. Hysterical! And *Taxi*. He and Rhea Pearlman made such a cute couple, didn't they? I mean—"

"Peggy. That's enough, please," said Tom. "I'm sure Mr. Drysdale doesn't want to hear this."

"Oh, that's okay," Drysdale chimed in. "I'm enjoying Peggy's stroll down memory lane. All those old TV shows. I think she's charming. Really."

Peggy turned around and stuck out her tongue at Tom. He gave her the finger. Drysdale turned and almost caught him in the act, but Tom swept his fingers through his hair just in time.

"Well, here we are," said Drysdale. "Just in the nick of time." The threesome entered the lavish conference room lined with floor to ceiling bookshelves, a large conference table, and plush leather chairs.

Tom spotted snarky Attorney Fred Kline along with several other people he didn't recognize. Drysdale made a sweeping motion to introduce the guests.

"Everyone, this is Tom Frye and his assistant, Peggy, here to notarize the documents. Tom, Peggy, Don Graybill."

Tom stepped forward and extended his hand. Graybill, average height and weight had thinning, brownish gray hair, complete with a side comb-over and a scraggly, droopy moustache. He wore faded blue jeans spotted with grease and dirt, and a black KISS tee shirt from a concert in 1978. Dirty steel-toed work boots completed his ensemble.

Graybill reached out with the calloused handshake of a hardworking man.

"Mr. Graybill, it's great to meet you, sir," Tom said. "This is my assistant, Peggy."

Right on cue, Peggy offered her hand to Graybill. She looked ready to faint. Graybill shook hands with her and turned to Tom.

"Hmmm, so you're Tom Frye? How do you know I'm Don Graybill?" he asked. "I mean, we've never met, right? How do you know I'm actually Graybill?" A long silence followed as he stared into Tom's eyes, waiting for an answer.

"Excuse me?" Tom turned to Drysdale, who wore a blank expression. Another awkward, long silence punctuated the room. Tom looked back at Attorney Kline, who smiled.

"Fred? Can you help me out here?"

Kline left his seat on the other side of the table and joined Tom, Peggy and Graybill. When he couldn't contain himself any more. He burst out laughing. "Okay, let's settle down now," he said. "Sorry about that. I'm afraid Mr. Graybill is having a little fun at your expense."

All the Graybill associates chuckled while Tom and Peggy looked at each other, confused.

Then Peggy giggled and broke the silence. She covered her mouth with her hand.

"Ha! Yeah, that's funny, isn't it?" Tom asked. "Are we ready to do some business? I don't want to take up any more of Mr. Graybill's time. Any more than we've already had to."

As the group arranged themselves around the table, Tom sensed Graybill's gaze boring into him. Already uncomfortable, Tom tried to smile and awaited further instruction.

"I'll ask you again, Frye. How do you know I'm really Don Graybill? Have we met before? Nope. So, *again*, how do you *know* I'm who I say I am?" Graybill stared at him, wearing his best poker face.

Tom looked from Kline to Drysdale for help. Kline smirked. Drysdale shrugged.

Speechless, Tom felt the beginnings of discomfort building in his bowels. *What the fuck?* With all eyes on him, he turned to Peggy, seated at his right hand, and threw up his hands in defeat.

Without missing a beat, Peggy turned and gave Graybill and his associates a big smile and giggled again. "Well, Mr. Graybill, I guess we're going to have to ask to see your driver's license. Or your passport if you'd prefer."

The room erupted in nervous laughter as Graybill reached into the back pocket of his dirty jeans and produced a Pennsylvania driver's license.

"Good thing you brought your girl along with you, Frye," Graybill said with a sarcastic smile. "I was losing patience."

Tom took a deep breath and looked at Peggy who tilted her head toward his briefcase. He removed the documents and slid them over to Graybill for signature. Peggy made goo-goo eyes at Graybill and notarized the documents when all signatures were completed.

Tom's stomach continued to churn and he felt the beginning of a migraine settling into his skull. An icepick of pain burrowed into the left side of his head. He twisted his wedding ring and tapped his foot to distract himself.

With the documents notarized, Tom hoped for a quick escape. Instead, Graybill invited everyone back to his private conference room for coffee. Tom's head pounded, yet he had no choice but to accept.

Peggy basked in the after-glow of her success, and lost all sense of restraint. She yapped with the handful of executives gathered in the office.

Tiny pangs of jealousy gnawed at Tom. She was really full of herself. He resented Peggy saving the day. In his mind she was subservient, less intelligent, and unsophisticated. But today she'd proved him wrong. These people loved her. So he stayed close to the refreshments, trying to look busy, sipping tepid coffee and nibbling a blueberry muffin he picked off the pastry tray.

He floated in and out of the conversations, like an out-of-body experience, catching snippets here and there. This foggy, dream-like state provoked his anxiety further. Tom looked into his hand and saw he had crumpled the paper napkin and the remainder of his muffin into a tight ball in his fist.

He looked for a waste basket to deposit the half-eaten muffin and sticky napkin, then tossed them into the trash. He needed to take another Valium or he would lose it. He turned his back, pulled the vial from his pocket and popped another pill. Certain no one had spotted him, he tried to relax and walked around the room.

Across the office, Peggy continued to chat with Drysdale and Graybill. She'd managed to enchant Graybill and his henchmen today. He didn't get it. *What could have them so interested?*

He tried to imagine how the others saw her. An attractive woman in her mid-thirties, mousy brown hair pulled into a low ponytail. Her best feature was her pale blue eyes, although they remained hidden by oversized glasses. And her taste in clothes sucked. Today, she wore non-descript beige polyester pants and a white striped blouse, with scuffed tan flats. But the thing that looked different about Peggy today? Today she was happy. That was the difference.

Attorney Kline walked over to Tom and started making chitchat about the success of their new profit-sharing plan. He bragged the new line of ergonomic office furniture was expected to send sales through the roof. Tom thought Kline was a fucking idiot—like most people who talk about things they know nothing about.

Nevertheless, Kline kept talking about the furniture, pointing out sample pieces scattered throughout the room. Tom nodded, pleased the Valium was kicking in.

Kline blathered about the "furniture of the future" and how employers owed it to their employees to protect their posture. *What a bunch of horseshit.* Bored, Tom nodded and smiled, uninterested in the sales pitch.

Then he noticed Drysdale and Graybill directing Peggy toward the display near the back of the conference room.

Although he couldn't hear them, it looked like they wanted Peggy to try out the furniture. Peggy sat in different chairs, tested a rocker, and then an Adirondack chair. She appeared to be enjoying herself. As she sat in the rocker she grinned broadly.

Tom kept spying, trying to imagine the conversation when he realized Kline had just asked him something. "I'm sorry, but what did you say?"

"Just asking if you were sure you wouldn't like to test any of the chairs? There's a nice selection over there. Looks like your secretary is enjoying herself." Annoyed, Tom again sighed. Kline was Graybill's attorney, not an actual employee of the company. *He shouldn't be forcing their furniture on anyone.*

"No, thanks. I leave the furniture buying to my wife. But I appreciate the offer. Actually, I think it's time Peggy and I got back to the office." Tom reached out to shake Kline's hand. He waved goodbye and walked over where Peggy sat rocking in the chair.

"Hey there. Ready to get back to the office?"

"Sure," Peggy said as she stood up. "We have to eventually." She smiled at Graybill and Drysdale. "Thanks so much," she said, shaking hands with the men. "For everything. It's been quite a day."

"It's been our pleasure," said Drysdale, who held on a little too long to Peggy's hand. "You must come back and visit and let us know how you like your present."

Peggy smiled and nodded her head. She released Drysdale's grip and turned to Graybill, "Thank you, Mr. Graybill."

"Nah! You earned it! Keeping that boss of yours in line," Graybill said. He gave Peggy an exaggerated wink and elbowed Drysdale with a chuckle.

"Excuse me," said Tom. "Present? Did you say present?"

Drysdale and Graybill exchanged a knowing glance but said nothing. Tom looked to Peggy for clarification.

"Peggy?"

Peggy blushed and looked to the men for the go ahead. Graybill flashed a thumbs up.

"Well," said Peggy. "The thing is..."

"We're giving Peggy the rocking chair," interrupted Graybill. "As a... token of our appreciation. We realize how she was put on the spot. Having to be ready at a moment's notice to notarize the documents for us—for the loan. Why, she told us she even had to pull you out of the dentist's chair today. The poor thing! My God, that's a lot of pressure. We just wanted to do a little something for her." Graybill stopped talking and folded his arms across his chest.

Tom was speechless. *Peggy had been inconvenienced? Are you joking? I was the one yanked out of a dentist appointment.*

"I'm sorry. What? You're giving *Peggy* a chair?" Tom asked.

"Yes, that's right," said Graybill. "Assuming you have no objections? She can take it with her today."

Tom blinked a few times, and tried to digest what was going on. *These people are giving Peggy a chair? And she's taking it with her? Today? What the hell?*

"Uh, objections? No, no, of course not," said Tom. "But I'm afraid it won't fit in my car. There isn't room for it, I mean."

"No problem," said Graybill. "We'll have it delivered. Peggy, just leave your address with the receptionist on your way out."

"Isn't that generous, Tom? They insisted!"

Tom, shocked from this latest development, tried to smile.

"Well, all right then," said Graybill. "Drysdale will see you out." Graybill started to walk away after shaking hands with Peggy and Tom, but then swung around. "Oh, Tom. I almost forgot. I have a little something for you too."

Tom got excited. *Wonder what it is? Maybe a desk? Or a cool ergonomic chair? Hopefully it isn't a rocking chair.* He wasn't a rocking chair guy. It could sure make up for the... what did they call it? Oh, yeah, the "inconvenience." *What a joke.*

"Hold on, now, I have it right here," said Graybill. He dug into the front pocket of his pants and pulled out something. "Yep. Here it is. Here ya go."

More confused than ever, Tom struggled to understand. *Where is my desk? Where is my chair? This can't be right.*

"Go on, man! Take it, don't be shy!" Graybill said.

Tom reached out to accept the gift. He looked down to process what was happening. He blinked. He swallowed hard. Then he opened his mouth to speak, but nothing came out.

There in the palm of his hand was a white Number 2 pencil with Graybill Industries written in bright red letters. Graybill slapped him on the back, smiled and walked away.

Tom said nothing, but tried to smile. He put the pencil in his shirt pocket.

Drysdale made a sweeping arm motion and looked eager to escort them out to reception.

"Ready to head out?"

Peggy nodded as she and Tom followed Drysdale. They retraced their steps and soon found themselves back at reception. Peggy stopped to give the receptionist her home address so the chair could be delivered. With a wave goodbye to Drysdale, they walked out the door and headed to the car.

Peggy opted not to talk, but instead cleared her throat a few times and blew her nose. Tom said nothing. The only sounds were their footsteps on the hot macadam parking lot, and the rustle as Peggy's polyester pants legs rubbed together.

Tom unlocked the doors, and they clicked their seatbelts when the engine started. He pulled his sunglasses from the visor on the driver's side and slid them to the end of his nose, then pulled the pencil out of his shirt pocket and examined it.

Obviously uncomfortable with the silence, Peggy attempted to pacify Tom. "Well, isn't that nice. A pencil! Those guys are really thoughtful."

Tom turned to Peggy, waved the pencil in front of her face, snapped it in two and threw it out the car window as he peeled out of the parking lot.

CHAPTER ELEVEN

The little car accident that landed Tom and Peggy in the emergency room shook everyone up. No one was hurt—except the Mercedes. Substantial damage to the front end summarized the accident report from the police. It remained unclear why or how Tom drove into the tree. Peggy explained they were merely on their way back to the office after the Graybill meeting.

The ER visit wrapped up quickly once the doctors determined no one was seriously hurt. No blood tests necessary, but the doctors suggested Tom get a stress test and take a vacation. The diagnosis looked like a good, old-fashioned panic attack.

Tom ignored the suggestion that he go home and take it easy for a few days. Instead he insisted Vicky take him to rent a car—another Mercedes—until his got out of the shop.

"You're not listening to any of the doctor's advice," Vicky said. "This is serious, Tom. You and Peggy could've been killed today."

"Yeah. No such luck, Vick," Tom said. "We're both still alive."

"Stop it. You're making me crazy. Fine. Go back and work yourself to death." She opened the door to get out, but Tom grabbed her arm and pulled her back inside.

"Okay, you win. I'll follow you back to the house."

"Good," Vicky smiled in victory. "You're a smart man after all." She leaned over and pecked a kiss on his cheek. "See you at home."

Tom seethed driving home. Peggy had saved the day. Her little "show me your driver's license" stunt nailed it. *Damn it!* If only he hadn't gotten so flustered. He should be pleased with his assistant. She'd used her instincts and it worked. She took control and used it to diffuse a tense situation. In this business, sometimes instincts were all you had to go on.

Tom knew Peggy could be an exceptional employee. In fact, he had told her at her last performance evaluation, if she put her mind to it, she could eventually advance to broker. He wished he had a female broker on his team. But Peggy imprisoned herself with mediocrity and complacency. She wanted the security of a regular paycheck, and she lacked the hunger needed to succeed. Today, she had showed a glimpse of her potential, which would likely remain untapped.

Despite objections from Vicky, Tom insisted on going back to work the next day. He'd addressed his morning anxiety by washing down a couple of Valium with his coffee. When he got to the office, he used the back entrance and avoided his co-workers. He walked straight into his office and shut the door; something he seldom did. He flopped down at his desk and let his head sink back into the chair. When he calmed down, he read his emails and sorted through the endless crap from "corporate" and the whiny emails from clients and coworkers. *Nothing urgent, thank God.*

His rumbling stomach reminded him he'd skipped breakfast. With his emails cleaned up, he could figure out what he wanted for lunch. He decided to treat himself at his favorite spot—Sushi Rob's. Located in the local downtown farmer's market, it amounted to a market stand with a few tiny tables and chairs.

For a while he had binged on sushi, going every day. His favorite, a special creation of the chef, had been named for him personally. Sushi Rob created a concoction of smoked salmon, cream cheese and sundried tomatoes called the "Sunny T." Now the chef and waitress called him "Sunny T" whenever he went to the restaurant. They even referred to Vicky as "Mrs. Sunny T." But she didn't like sushi. Instead she would walk over to the seafood stand for a crab cake sandwich. Now, Tom went for sushi alone. He enjoyed talking to Sushi Rob almost as much as the food.

Tom considered himself a student of human behavior. Thus, his clients provided most of the data for his observations. For years he'd catered to the whims of rich, ego-driven clients. But, in Sushi Rob, Tom found someone who represented a break from the demands of his clients.

From what he had observed, a sushi chef seldom interacted with the customers. They prepared their dishes with an almost somber demeanor. Even in an empty restaurant, the sushi chef remained at his station, chopping and prepping for the next customer. Although Tom never sat at the "sushi bar" himself, he thought the interaction between customer and chef looked minimal.

However, Sushi Rob was different. Rob chatted with his customers. He remembered his regular patrons and their preferences. He knew who liked extra wasabi or ginger, or which folks preferred brown rice for their rolls. In particular, he enjoyed whipping out his mini-blowtorch to "cook" anything a customer didn't want to eat raw. The blowtorch always cracked Tom up; it reminded him of the ones those chefs on television use when they're preparing crème brûlée.

A small wiry man, Rob looked strong and fit. His white chef hat hid much of his face, except for a shock of straight, coal black hair peeking out that hid his dark eyes. Tom liked and admired Sushi Rob the most because he had such a great rapport with his customers. He always cracked jokes and charmed them with his antics.

Their odd friendship started when Tom fantasized about inventing a wasabi-flavored potato chip. Tom loved wasabi, and no matter how much was on his sushi, he always wanted a little more. The idea came one day at the farmer's market when he bought a bag of Martins' Kettle Cooked chips to go with his "Sunny T" lunch. Tom loved the combination of salt, flavor and crunch. Sushi Rob and his helper found it hilarious that Tom would corrupt an otherwise healthy lunch by adding chips.

"No one eats chips with sushi, Sunny T," Sushi Rob said. "This would be blasphemy in my country. No one would eat this combination!"

Tom had no clue which country Sushi Rob was from. *Maybe the Philippines?* Wherever it was, Tom had a hunch they weren't known for sushi. Intuition sent a shiver up his spine.

"But chips are delicious with everything," said Tom. "Chips are the best food in the world—next to chocolate. Well, and the 'The Sunny T'."

"I'm not so sure, about that," Sushi Rob said. "You not be popular man in my country if you seen in public eating chips with sushi." Sushi Rob scowled, teasing Tom. "You must be very, very careful not to anger chef. Especially one holding sharp knife!"

"Okay. I promise next time I won't get the chips. But Rob, if you could find a way to pump wasabi into potato chips, we could make a fortune. I know it."

The wasabi chip matter dropped for the time being, but Tom still thought the idea had real potential. He continued to have chips with his sushi—just not in front of Rob. He brought them from home, took his sushi to-go, and ate them together on the sly at his desk.

Six months later, Tom noticed a headline in the newspaper that caught his attention: "Lays Potato Chips to add new Wasabi Chip to its Line." When Tom waved the newspaper in front of him, Rob raised an eyebrow from beneath his chef's hat and smiled.

Although most days he now took his sushi back to the office, Tom sometimes sat at one of the tiny tables in the marketplace to talk to Rob. They discussed a wide variety of topics ranging from politics to sports, children and even financial strategies. One of Rob's more interesting stories evolved around his "accountant."

"Sunny T," Rob said one afternoon, "You should really meet my accountant, Hung Lo. He's Chinese—not from Philippines like me, but he is 'The Man' in Cray Asian community. Very smart—saves lots of money for us. You should meet. I need to swing by his place after work tonight. You want to come along?"

Rob finished Tom's roll and handed it over.

"Hmmm, Hung Lo? Seriously? That's the guy's name? You're kidding, right?"

"No, that's his name, man, Hung Lo. Comes from a very honorable Chinese family. Very old and distinguished name in China," said Rob.

"Wow. So he's actually from China? That's very cool."

"No, man. He's from New Jersey," said Sushi Rob. "Bayonne, I think. Not sure. But you should meet, Sunny T. Very well connected. Asian people very clever with money, you know? Get new customers."

Tom turned to leave when he saw a police officer walking toward the stand. The cop held up his wrist, pointing to his watch when he made eye contact with Rob.

Rob nodded, put down his knife, removed his gloves and rummaged around in his pants pocket. He pulled out a set of keys and held them up.

"Sunny T, can you move my car for me? I'm in no-parking zone. Cop not happy. Can you move into parking lot for me?"

Rob tossed the keys to Tom, who caught them just before they hit the ground. "What?" Tom said.

"Right out front. My car. Little MG. Red. You can't miss it. Thanks. Just park it over behind market in parking lot. Should be empty now."

Sushi Rob got back to work and Tom left to find the red MG. He chuckled to himself, surprised that Rob would ask him to help. Within a few moments, he located the tiny car—a fiery red two-seater, and crawled in. He tried to find room for his lunch on the passenger seat, but restaurant supplies littered the car.

God, this is so small. How does he fit in here with his wife and little boy? Not to mention, there is no sign of a car seat. Disturbed, Tom moved the car over to the lot behind the market and walked back inside to return Rob's keys.

"Thanks, man," Rob said. "I owe you—free roll tomorrow—but anyway, how about tonight? You come with me to meet Hung Lo? What time you finished work? I told him around six."

Tom thought for a moment about his schedule. *I've got nothing going on after five. No family obligations. What the hell? Vicky won't care. I can call when I get back to the office.*

"Yeah, sure. Why not?" Tom said. "Meet you in the parking lot about six?"

"Good," Rob said. "You not be disappointed!"

On the walk back to the office, Tom smirked thinking about Hung Lo. *I wonder if he's really an accountant? Oh well. If nothing else, it's a change of pace.*

Back at the office, Tom had just settled in to eat his lunch when Lance ruined everything. Knocking, he stuck his fat head inside the door. *Great.* The sight of Lance's enormous bulbous head and his beady little eyes squinting through smudged glasses made Tom's skin crawl.

"Hey! What's up?" Lance asked.

"Nothing," Tom said, further annoyed. "What's up with you?"

"Just wanted to see how you guys made out yesterday, that's all," Lance said. "If this is a bad time, we can talk later." He flashed a sheepish grin.

"Not much to talk about," Tom said. "Everything's wrapped up."

"Huh," snickered Lance, "that's funny, because Peggy seems full of herself out here." Lance pointed in the direction of their assistant. "She said you owe her big time... that she saved the day for you."

"Yeah, well that's Peggy for you. Always trying to get brownie points for doing her job. She notarized documents. Period. End of story." Without further comment, Tom broke eye contact with Lance and turned his attention to his computer.

"Well I hate to break it to you, buddy, but that's not the way she tells the story. I mean, she said—"

"Jesus, Lance. What's your problem? You trying to rub my nose in this? You've gotta lot of nerve, and I don't have time for this shit right now."

"Oh, hey man. Sorry. No offense intended. Honest. Um, I guess I'll talk to you later then," Lance stammered as he closed the door behind him.

Tom fumed and felt his blood pressure climbing. He pushed his chair away from the desk and stood up, taking deep even breaths, just like his doctor told him.

"Fuck!" he screamed and slammed his fist on the desk. Immediately, his phone intercom interrupted his tantrum.

"You okay in there, boss?" Peggy chuckled. "Do you need help? With something else?"

"Go to hell!" he screamed, but realized he was acting childish. "Sorry. No, I don't need anything. Thanks." Tom clicked the intercom off and put his head down on the desk. Moments later, Peggy called on the intercom again. Tom slammed his fist once more.

"Peggy, what is it now?"

"Sorry to bother you again, but Jack Burke is holding on line four for you."

"Double fuck," Tom said and turned off the intercom. Within seconds, Peggy transferred Jack Burke, his funeral director client through.

Well, here we go again. So much for having an early lunch.

Tom mentally prepared for the conversation with Jack Burke, a nice, albeit boring man. Not a shock if you considered all the time the guy spent with the dead. He even looked like a funeral director—tall and slender with thinning gray hair and impeccably dressed. Tom appreciated Jack's sense of style, since he had little tolerance for professional people who didn't dress well.

That reminds me, I need to talk to Lance. He looks sloppier than ever these days.

Tom forced himself to focus as he picked up the phone. "Jack, how are you?"

"I hope I'm not interrupting your lunch?" Jack said.

Tom's stomach rumbled loudly. "No, of course not. What's up?"

"Well, I wanted to see if you might be able to stop over to the house sometime this week? I've got some questions about my mother's will... some of the assets. I think they're supposed to be transferred to my boy, Leon. As a condition of the estate."

"Sure. I'll transfer you back out to Peggy to set something up. I'll see you soon, Jack."

"Great. Thanks, Tom."

"Bye, Jack."

Tom redirected the call back to Peggy. He needed to review the conditions of the estate, and the distribution of assets before the meeting.

Tom recalled Leon as a deadbeat who lived with his grandmother, the elder Mrs. Burke. Over the years he'd heard complaints that Leon was a slacker and freeloader. He'd barely graduated from college and now tried to make a living as a substitute gym teacher. His parents described him as a young man with a failure to launch—a phrase Tom found comical. Leon had gotten a gig as a long-term sub, but had been accused of inappropriate contact with a couple of male students.

Something clicked in Tom's brain. *That story about the molested boys. Oh, shit! Those are the boys Marcia came to me about.*

Now he remembered everything. He had heard rumors that two boys had been injured while "wrestling" after school with Coach Leon, and the one had to be "hospitalized briefly."

Well, Jesus. This is awkward. Do I need to talk to Jack about this?

Tom wondered over the years why Leon hadn't gotten into the family business. But this explained a lot. He preferred the living—little boys—to corpses. It would've been easy to fall into the family business, at least as some sort of assistant. One of those people who stuck the funeral flags on the cars going to the cemetery, or one of those polite but serious people who handed out the programs at the celebration of life ceremonies.

Tom had met Jack's mother, Mrs. Burke several times. She lived in a little house next to the workshop where Jack did his embalming and the other work. The business compound included a small cottage, the workshop and a big brick building where the visitations and viewings occurred.

A third-generation funeral director, Jack operated a successful business. His grandfather had been a small town undertaker but grew the business over the years. Now the family lived in a much larger private residence about a half mile down the private road on 100 acres of prime real estate.

Tom hadn't visited the Burke compound for a while. The place gave him the creeps, and not just the funeral parlor. The entire house reeked of bad taste, courtesy of Burke's second wife Joy.

A plump, pushy woman with a poufy '80's hairdo, Joy had married Jack when the boys were in their late teens. She was a friendly woman who gestured wildly with her doughy white hands when she talked. Once she had bopped Tom on the cheek when telling one of her exaggerated stories. Her life revolved around spending her husband's money, and the horses she boarded on the property. Childless, her horses were her babies.

Tom heard his stomach rumbling again—a reminder his lunch sat in front of him on the desk. Exhausted from the day, he started to unwrap the roll, and then changed his mind. He put it down, walked over to his office door, opened it a crack and called out, "Peggy, I'm going to eat lunch. Hold my calls, okay?" She didn't answer. He opened the door wide, but no sign of her. She must've gone to lunch too. *The calls will just have to go to voicemail. Besides, Lance is probably lurking around somewhere. He can answer the office lines. Anyone who needs me will track me down one way or another.*

Tom wolfed down his sushi. After a few belches, he patted his stomach in appreciation. Now drowsy, he yawned and stretched back in his chair. *God, I could use a nap. But do I risk it at work?*

He opened the door again and stuck his head out. It looked like the place was empty. There was no sign of Peggy or anyone else. He closed and locked the door, and pulled down the window shades. *Christ, this is weird. I never lock my door. Well, except that time Vicky and I came back here after happy hour that one night...* He smiled at the memory.

He kicked off his wingtips, put his feet up on the desk, leaned back and closed his eyes. Then he decided he should set an alarm—just in case—so he pulled out his phone, settled for twenty minutes, and closed his eyes.

The next thing he knew, his legs cramped and he tried to stretch them out. *Ugh, not a charlie horse. Wow, my legs really hurt. And what is that noise?* He tried to stretch out, but in Sushi Rob's small car his legs smashed against the dashboard.

It was so dark driving through the city neighborhoods. *Where are we? Nothing looks familiar. Is this Cray? I've never been here before.* Sketchy looking teenagers collected on the street corners like fireflies attracted to the light from the buzzing streetlights. The streets rang with laughter and what sounded like gunshots. Tom jumped in his seat, startled from the noise, but then realized Rob's car had backfired. Rob laughed and slapped his arm.

As they drove, Tom's senses were on high alert. He saw a couple of young men skateboarding on a homemade wooden ramp, next to low-income housing units. Laughter intermingled with the crash and whir when skateboard wheels hit the pavement. A tickle of fear crept into the pit of his stomach and he swallowed hard to keep his composure. His hands began to sweat.

"Where are we, Rob? I don't recognize anything around here."

"Huh! No shit, man. We're in Chinatown, Sunny T. Hung Lo's neighborhood. Hang tight. Almost there." Rob's dark eyes flashed in the green glow of the car's interior dashboard lights. "You're not scared are you?"

Rob laughed and pulled over in front of an Asian market. A large black and red neon sign above the door read in English and Chinese "Wong Fat's Chinese Market." The building, a massive, three-story brick unit appeared to have an apartment above the store. A black wrought-iron fence enclosed a tiny yard with a few splotches of grass. A cracked sidewalk ran the length of a ragged clothesline strung up between two trees.

"Come on, this is it," said Rob. "We park here. His place is in basement. Down the steps, over there."

Rob pointed to a set of stairs along the side of the building that led to Hung Lo's place. They walked over to the dark stairway, dimly lit by an outdoor light at the top of the steps. Tom followed Rob down the cement staircase, gripping the metal handrail.

"Hey, Rob. Does Hung Lo know you're bringing me along?"

"Ha! No, Sunny T! Hung Lo love surprises!"

Tom offered a weak smile. "Great."

As they climbed down the steps, the smell of damp concrete made Tom's eyes water and his nose tickle. Cold sweat ran down his back between his shoulder blades. At the bottom of the dimly lit entrance, Rob rang the doorbell and somebody buzzed them in.

Rob opened the door to a huge cloud of cigarette smoke. Through the pall Tom saw a large round Asian man sitting at a desk, leaning back in his chair. He had long black hair, slicked back, and an unfiltered cigarette dangled from plump lips under a full, black moustache. Glasses attached to one of those funky beaded chains dangled at the end of his nose. He operated a calculator, in the middle of tallying something, with a huge stack of file folders piled in front of him. Perched next to him was a beautiful, exotic dark-haired woman on top of the desk, her long legs crossed and dangling. She wore short shorts, high-heeled platform sandals and a skimpy tank top. Her full breasts looked ready to explode from underneath the gauzy material.

Never intimidated, Rob barged in with Tom trailing a few steps behind. "Hung Lo! Meet Sunny T, 'The Money Man!' The guy I tell you about, you know? He's a regular Mr. Stocks and Bonds."

Tom stepped forward and offered a tentative handshake to Hung Lo, whose hands were crispy and dry like old paper.

"Nice to meet you," Tom said.

Hung Lo said nothing in return. He looked at Rob and pointed to the woman on his desk. "You meet Bindy? Last time you were here?"

"Yeah, yeah, I think. This is my friend, Sunny T, Tom Frye."

Bindy, who looked bored, smiled and nodded to the men before she stood up to walk over to a large metal coffee pot in the corner of the room. Noisily, she clanged china cups and opened drawers.

Hung Lo ground out his cigarette in the overflowing ashtray on his desk and immediately lit another. Tom started to cough. Hung Lo acted annoyed and stared at him.

"So, Hung Lo," said Rob, "I thought I would bring Tom—Sunny T—to come meet you. I told him how you help Asian community here in Cray. Maybe you can work together, share some clients? Eh? You know... like referrals and shit? That's what you call it, right? You and Sunny T, help each other?"

Again, Hung Lo said nothing and stared straight ahead. He glanced between Rob and Tom, squinting his eyes as he puffed on his cigarette.

Off in the distance, a ruckus developed. It sounded like crowing chickens and people shouting.

"Sounds like a barnyard," Tom said without thinking. He regretted it when Hung Lo whirled around in his chair and then stood up.

"What are you thinking, man? Bringing him here tonight? You forget about the cock fighting at 8:00? You better get the fuck out of here before things get started. Not unless you're willing to place a bet and stick around."

Rob stayed calm and slapped Tom on the back. "Shit, man! We gonna stay for the fight. You think I forget?" Rob kept smiling and put his arm around Tom's shoulders. "He's cool, Hung Lo, no problem. Probably got lots of cash, too. Right, Sunny T?"

Too stunned to say anything, Tom looked back and forth between the two men. He opened his mouth to speak, but nothing came out. Meanwhile a door across the room opened to reveal another room beyond. Tom saw a dozen or so people milling around—mostly men, as far as he could tell.

Sushi Rob pushed him through the smoky haze and toward the other room. He smiled and urged Tom forward, but Tom's feet stayed planted in the floor, like they were rooted in sludge.

Hung Lo continued to glare while his cigarette bobbed up and down. Tom couldn't look away from the fiery glow of its ember. *Is he talking to me? His lips are moving, but I can't hear him.*

Rob continued to urge him toward the back room. Tom willed his feet to move, and finally walked across the room toward the open door. A loud roaring formed in his ears, and now he clearly heard squawking. *Nah, it's more like the sound a rooster makes in the morning: "Cock-a-doodle-doo!" Is my mind playing tricks?* He thought he heard rustling feathers, and imagined their sharp hackles.

The noise continued to build like a crescendo in the smoky haze as he struggled to lift his feet. He heard shouts and laughter and the clinking of glass bottles, and he swore he heard someone counting out money, like the sound of crisp bills passing between dirty fingers. *Are people placing bets? Is that what that is?*

Closer now, he looked up and thought he saw a swirl of golden red feathers floating up toward the low drop ceiling. He heard the clanking of metal cages opening and closing as the birds were released. The crowd gathered around a center ring where handlers attended to two large birds.

One was brown, tinged with red and white, while the other was all black except for red feathers on top of its head. The handlers attached tiny cuffs with miniature scythes to the birds' legs. The sharp weapons glinted under the fluorescent lights.

Tom called out, "Rob, what's happening? Why are we here for this? I thought we were here to talk about business referrals... accounting... sharing clients. I don't want to be here. I need to leave—right now. I could lose my license if anyone sees me here!"

Everyone laughed, pointing and snickering. They threw back their heads and laughed out loud. *My God, it's like these people can read my mind. I'm so afraid.*

"Oh, Sunny T," Rob said with a smile. "You didn't think he was real accountant, did you? Hung Lo is different—you know, like a bookie. Cock fighting very popular in Philippines, Sunny T. Very ancient sport. Makes big money. Hung Lo is the man! Very successful—just maybe not what you expect, eh?"

"I'm sorry, man, but I gotta go." Tom turned to leave but again his feet wouldn't move. He struggled and tried to turn, but it was so hard to walk. The smoke made him feel dizzy and a little nauseous, and the laughter from the crowd intimidated him. He needed to leave.

"Sunny T," Rob said. "How you getting home? You rode here with me. Remember?"

"I'll call a taxi," Tom said. "It'll be fine, I'll call a cab."

Now, everyone in the place laughed at Tom, pointing their fingers, drinking their bottles of beer and laughing.

"Cab! Ha, ha!" Rob said. "That's funny, Sunny T. No cabs come into Chinatown. Not this time of night! You not going anywhere."

Tom's heart pounded as he reached for his cell phone to call for help. No signal. The crowd laughed as he struggled to get to the door. Several women reached out and began to touch him, pulling on his arms, trying to persuade him to stay. He broke away and kept walking toward the doorway. *Almost there.* Then the cool metal of the doorknob turned in his hand and the door opened.

The chilly evening breeze blew on his sweaty face and he pulled out his phone again, praying he had a signal. *Finally.* He started to dial 911 for help, when the unmistakable feel of the cold steel barrel of a gun pointed into the back of his head. He heard a loud click, and then nothing.

The sonar chime on his phone kept ringing as Tom bolted upright in his chair. He looked around the room, his breath coming in hard loud gasps. His head was splitting. Disoriented, he turned off the alarm. *Oh, shit. I'm at the office.*

For a moment he did nothing but gaze around, trying to calm down. It was only a nightmare. He remembered now. He'd decided to take a nap, and must've fallen asleep and had that awful dream. Thank God. He let out a long, deep breath and walked over to his windows to open the shades.

He walked to the door and opened it a crack. *Yep, there's Peggy, back from lunch.* He heard Lance blabbing to someone down the hall.

Peggy looked up from her computer and slid her glasses to the end of her nose. "Hey, are you okay?"

"Yeah. Fine. Thanks," Tom said. "Just tired." Leaving the door open, he walked back to his desk and sat down.

He took another deep breath, scrolled through the contact list on his phone and dialed. Ringing, ringing, ringing. *Ah, finally.* Tom listened to the voicemail prompt and left a message.

"Rob? Hey, it's Tom Frye. Sunny T. Looks like I'm not gonna to be able to make it tonight after all."

CHAPTER TWELVE

Tom had seen a lot of tacky, over the top decorating in his day. Clients—especially the nouveau riche had a heavy-handed decorating style.

As Jack Burke greeted him and led him into the foyer, Tom saw the single most obnoxious thing he'd ever seen in a client's home—an unidentified large image inlaid in the hardwood floor of the Burkes' foyer.

At first he questioned what he saw. He stared at the elaborate patterns, but couldn't quite make out the design in the dead center of the floor. He circled around the outer edge of it, stopping to pause, hoping to gain a different perspective.

Joy Burke made her entrance down the large curved staircase. "Tom, you look confused. Did you figure it out? It's a horse's head."

"Oh. Right," Tom said. "Now I get it."

"Tom, you know Joy," Jack gestured, hands sweeping toward the equine-themed décor. "She had an artist sketch her horse Betsy, and put our flooring professional to work."

Tom stared at the floor again, intrigued yet revolted by this display. He wasn't an animal lover, and he struggled around people who gushed about their pets. Plus he hadn't ridden a horse since he was a little boy, and that had been a frightening experience.

At his friend's eighth birthday party, the horse Tom had ridden galloped wildly and didn't heed his timid commands. Although exaggerated over the years, the memory still made his pulse race when he thought about the crazy animal tearing around the dirt trail. It had terrified him, convinced he'd be thrown. His friends laughed and snickered when Bucky the horse tossed him around like a ragdoll.

Tom realized Joy had asked him something. "I'm sorry, what did you say?"

"I asked if you'd like to meet Betsy—in person?" Joy repeated.

"Betsy? Is that your daughter?"

"What? No! It's my horse," Joy said, looking annoyed and shaking her blonde bob.

"Oh. That's nice of you, but not today, maybe another time?"

"Sure," Joy said. "Any time." She excused herself and walked back up the elaborate staircase. "Well, I need to get back to my chores. Nice to see you, Tom."

He watched her chubby figure climb the steps and disappear.

"Let's go into the den, so we can talk." Jack waved Tom into an office to the right of the large foyer.

They sat down and made small talk as Tom produced a thick pack of legal documents. When they started reviewing the forms, he noticed Jack was crying. Always uncomfortable with tears, particularly those of his male clients, Tom didn't know what he should do next. *If I pat him on the back, I'll have to stand up, walk over there and stand over him. God, this is so awkward.*

He tried to channel his "Inner Vicky." *She's always better in weird, uncomfortable situations like this. She's the one who majored in communications.*

He didn't know what else to do, so he blurted out the first thing that came into his mind when he saw Jack wiping his nose with the back of his shirt sleeve. "Jesus, aren't there any tissues in here?"

Jack glared at the insensitive comment.

Tom immediately realized his *faux pas*. "There are never any tissues around when you need one. That's all I meant. Should I go out and buy you some?" Tom stammered, struggling to smooth things over with his distraught client. He readjusted the stack of papers in front of him.

Without comment, Jack reached down and produced a small cube of tissues from inside the desk drawer and dropped them in front of Tom. He pulled one out and blew, honking and wiping his eyes. Surprisingly, this calmed him down. He'd stopped crying—for the moment.

Damn. I need to invest more money in Kleenex.

Tom zeroed in on this new opportunity to appear helpful. He smiled and leaned in, moving his chair a bit closer.

"Jack, do you want to keep going with this paperwork?"

Jack stared at him for a minute, and then spoke quietly, "I've been under so much stress. I don't know where to start." He wiped his eyes and continued. "I don't think my mother's death was an accident. I think she was murdered." Jack deposited the dirty tissue in the trashcan. "And I think my son Leon is the one who killed her."

A long silence echoed in the office.

Jack swallowed hard, but didn't speak. He finally cleared his throat. "Leon was there—with mom, you know—in the house, when she died and..."

Tom didn't move. Didn't comment. Only stared in disbelief.

Jack continued his story. "Well. Look. You knew Leon had been staying with mom, right? For eighteen months. It was only supposed to be for a short time, but here we are." Jack cleared this throat several times and sniffed.

Leon. In trouble again.

As a very dedicated financial advisor, Tom was privy to a slew of sensitive information. He made it his business to know which clients' children had been to rehab, and which had messy or multiple divorces. He knew those with estranged relatives reappearing to borrow money, or threatening blackmail if their wealthy siblings wouldn't bail them out of jail.

Tom nodded and Jack continued, "After that trouble with the school district a while back, you remember?" Jack's voice dropped to a whisper. "When he was accused of... you know, with the wrestlers?"

Jesus H. Christ. How could I forget? Tom wrung his hands on the desktop.

"I was on his back to get out on his own. I thought he needed to leave town and start fresh somewhere else." Jack stopped talking and twisted the tissue in his hand.

"I'm not sure I understand, Jack. Your mother was almost ninety years old. Did they argue? Did she threaten to kick him out?"

"Not exactly. Leon knew I stood to inherit the bulk of her estate since I was Mom's only child. But as *my* only child, Leon was named in the will for a substantial sum. My mother told me she was leaving the house to him but I was against it."

Entertaining young boys, probably.

"I'm pretty sure he was abusing, or at least using painkillers—Oxy, maybe others, I don't know. He helped Mom lay out her pills every night before she went to bed."

How thoughtful. Ha! One for you and two for me...

"Joy and I were concerned he wasn't being careful enough, but Mom didn't see it that way. She trusted him. But the pharmacy, and her doctor too, called me. They were concerned she was taking too much of her medication. Leon had tried refilling some of the scripts too soon—the painkillers."

Jack paused and blew his nose again, then took a sip of water.

"She had chronic back pain. Kept her practically bedridden. So the prescriptions were legitimate. I told the doctor she was confused, so he bought the story, but after that I counted her pills." He chuckled and then choked back a sob. "She told me to mind my own business."

Tears leaked from his eyes again.

"She liked having Leon keep her company. And she became more dependent on him. Still, Joy and I did all her shopping, and drove her to her appointments. But the pills, I don't know. I never confronted him. I had my suspicions. There were times when he acted out of it. But I didn't smell alcohol on his breath."

Denial. Denial. Denial. Oh, denial is bad.

"A few weeks ago when I dropped off Mom's groceries, I found some pills in an unmarked bottle. I asked Leon about it, but he mumbled something and told me to 'fuck off.' I pocketed one and took it down to the pharmacy to identify it. I didn't want to believe he would deliberately kill his own grandmother. But... I'm pretty sure he did."

Great. A pervert and a murderer.

An uncomfortable silence continued to gain momentum. Tom cleared his throat and stood up to walk around the room.

This kid lost his teaching job because of the wrestling scandal. He couldn't keep a job so he sponged off his grandmother. And now his father thinks he killed her. Christ. This makes Marcia look like a girl scout.

What could Tom say that wouldn't seem like a line of bull? His pulse raced and his mouth was dry. He looked at the buffet table in the office, the one with a pitcher of water. He willed himself to get out of the chair to get a drink. He needed another pill.

"Jack, could I get some water? I'm parched."

"Sure, Tom. I should've offered." While Jack walked over to the buffet table and filled a glass, Tom used the opportunity to fish another Valium out of his vial and pop it in his mouth. He swallowed the pill and guzzled the entire glass of water when Jack brought it over.

"Thanks. Sorry, I'm a little dehydrated, I guess." Tom found it difficult to make full eye contact, and waited for a revelation about what he should do next.

Okay, God. What do I do now? This is bad. A murder confession? I can't fix this.

Tom looked down at the floor and scanned the silent room. In the distance, a grandfather clock chimed the hour.

Jack stared at Tom, bending his head, trying to force eye contact. He began to pace around the room, alternating between wringing his hands and running his fingers through his hair. Then something dark clouded over his eyes.

"Tom, I apologize. You don't need to hear about this. I'm letting my imagination run wild. Forget I ever said anything. Mom lived a long life, and in this line of work, I've seen my share of untimely deaths." Jack gave Tom a sideways glance, as if trying to gauge if he'd convinced him.

Quick, think! Remember why you're here.

"Jack, I'm sure you're tired. I've got all the documents you need right here. They're ready to go. All you have to do is sign." Tom forced himself to smile, but his hands were shaking. "Make sure you take this whole packet with you when you go to Attorney Doyle's office. In fact, I can help. Let's finish up this paperwork now. We'll get a couple of signatures and I'll get out of your hair. I'll drop these over to Doyle for you myself. I'm seeing him day after tomorrow."

Jack nodded in agreement and sat back in his chair. He signed the forms and Tom headed toward the door. Out of the corner of his eye Tom spotted the gaudy horse head design in the hardwood floor again. He paused and turned back toward his client. "Jack, don't get up. I'll see myself out. I'll tell Doyle to call me if he has any questions. We'll talk soon."

Before his client could say a word, Tom walked through the foyer and out the front door. He paused and waved.

Poor bastard. His problems are just getting started.

CHAPTER THIRTEEN

By the time Tom got home, his imagination ran wild with theories about Jack's son killing Mrs. Burke. He tried not to stereotype people, but Leon—unemployed most of the time—fit the description of a deadbeat. Leon alternated between milking the state's unemployment compensation program and his sporadic substitute-teaching career. The part-time wrestling coach assignments only contributed to a very sketchy work history.

But why had Jack told Tom about his suspicions? A nagging hunch said Jack spilled his guts because he had no close friends to confide in. His need for privacy and his embarrassment made it difficult to share. Thus, Tom made a good candidate.

Vicky greeted him with a hug when he walked into the kitchen. She turned and grabbed an envelope off the kitchen counter and waved it in his face.

"Hey babe, what's up?" he asked and planted a kiss on her cheek.

"Two words for you, mister," she said. "Jury duty."

Tom hurled his briefcase on the ground, loosened his tie and ripped open the envelope. "Seriously? Again? What the fuck? I just had jury duty!" Tom got the feeling she'd baited him.

"Four years ago," Vicky said. "Technically they can call you every three. You got a break, an extra year off." She winked.

"And in federal court? They could hold me hostage for weeks. Months even."

The Pennsylvania legal system had very strict rules for potential jurors, so Tom figured the federal judicial system had to be worse. No cell phones, no newspapers, no magazines, and even if they decided to excuse you, they kept you locked up in the courthouse for a full week, excepting forty-five minutes for lunch. The thought of federal jury duty caused a complete meltdown.

"Well, that's just great," he said. "I can't afford to be off work for a whole week again. No phone, no Internet. Jesus! There's gotta be a way to get out of this. I'm gonna call Doyle." Tom knew Doyle was skilled at finagling people out of their obligations—legal or otherwise.

"Yeah, well, good luck with that, hon," Vicky said. "I don't think Doyle is going to be able to come to your rescue for this one. But go ahead and call him. I'll start dinner."

"I'm calling right now. It's been radio silence from him the past couple of days. Besides, I need to talk to him about another client." Grabbing a Heineken out of the fridge, Tom chugged some of it before calling Doyle.

As Vicky had predicted, Doyle laughed long and hard. "Hahahaha! Sucks to be you, FRYEMAN!" Doyle screamed Tom's old frat nickname into the phone. "FREAKIN' FRYEMAN! ASSHOLE!"

"Jesus, just stop it. This is not funny! Do you realize how difficult this situation is for me? To be out of contact with my clients, my office, for God knows how long? I'll be separated from my livelihood, incommunicado from the pulse of my work."

"Relax, asshole. It's jury duty—not a life sentence in prison. It's one of those things you're going to have to suck-up and deal with. A couple of weeks, and you'll be good as new—like it never happened."

Silence lingered on both ends of the line. Tom continued pouting silently, and pictured Doyle covering the phone with his hand, stifling a laugh into his elbow.

Finally, Doyle picked up where he left off. "Look, man. I'm really sorry, but honestly, this is not something I can fix for you. Federal jury duty is nothing to fuck with. A speeding ticket, prostitution, hell, even a DUI, and I'm your Mr. Fix It, but this? No way, bro. You've gotta face the music. Sorry."

Tom didn't take the news well. Instead, he made a loud huffing noise. "Yeah, well fuck you, anyway." He hung up the phone.

"That sounded productive—and mature," Vicky called from the kitchen.

Tom stormed in and hurled his empty beer bottle into the recycling bin. He rummaged in the fridge, found another and gulped it as he watched his smirking wife.

"Thomas," Vicky said. "Really? Come on, honey. Don't be so angry. It's only a week. And the office can run without you." She put her arms around his shoulders from behind and gave him a squeeze. "I'm more worried you'll put off the vacation you've been promising me. Come on, let's find something to do with all that energy. You can help me pack up the stuff for the Salvation Army that I put in the garage."

Tom finished the rest of his beer with a long chug, tossed it in the trash and started walking upstairs. "Okay, Vick. I'll be right there after I change clothes."

Once Tom accepted his pending jury duty, the weekend passed without incident. Vicky put Tom and the girls to work cleaning out the garage and loading up boxes of unwanted stuff to give to charity. Over the years, so much junk had accumulated—old toys, toddler-sized clothes, equipment from every sport imaginable, games, old appliances, vacation souvenirs and books, books, and more books.

He didn't like housework, but he morphed into a cleaning machine once he got started. He classified most things as unnecessary, so every mismatched game piece, ragged stuffed animal, or naked Barbie doll, was banished and ceremoniously earmarked for the trash or the Salvation Army.

Although he knew they worked for some people, he hated yard sales and consignment stores. But he wanted things removed from his environment. He threw everything away, and his family knew it. Landfills didn't concern him. Even the garbage men complained every week that he put out too much trash.

When his wife's parents moved ten years ago from their single-family home, Tom led the charge to de-clutter. They continued to blame him when something went missing. *"Tom must've thrown it away,"* his mother-in-law would say.

Usually he had.

"Why would anyone want to keep electronic television tubes from the 1950s and '60s, or an old, black rotary telephone?" he asked Vicky.

"I don't know," she answered. "But my sister is convinced you threw away tons of valuable stuff when Mom and Dad moved to Country Acres."

"Yeah, maybe. But who in the hell has time to research whether your childhood 'Light Bright' is valuable on eBay? I mean, for crying out loud, Vick, I was trying to help."

"Ha. I know. It was only after you threatened to rent a dumpster and start pitching stuff that they threw anything away."

Tom laughed at this, but felt vindicated when he recalled all the crap they'd had to pitch. Golf clubs, old broken appliances, A.M. clock radios, ancient electronics and a large box of cheap Christmas decorations were only a few of the mementoes that cluttered the family homestead.

"Well, I did them a huge favor. That house was a fire hazard."

"Yeah, well I'm still waiting for you to get rid of your own junk. The cannon ball..."

"My Civil War collectibles aren't junk, Vick. You know that. Someday those rifles are going to be worth a ton of money. In fact, they already are. Maybe I'll sell something."

"I've heard that before. I still remember when the kids were bowling with the cannon ball in the basement that time..."

"All right. Enough. I get it."

***

Tom hated to admit it, but cleaning out the old junk in the garage had cheered him up. It fueled his desire for control, and helped purge his anxiety. Best of all, he recovered from his summons for jury duty. He even managed to act nice when he saw Peggy and Lance at the office Monday morning.

"Good morning," he said. "Everybody have a good weekend?"

"Well, I suppose," Lance said. "Although, my son got stranded with a flat tire on Friday night, and I had to—"

"Yeah, tough break," Tom interrupted. "Well, anyway, time to see what came in over the weekend."

Back in his office, he rummaged through the stack of mail.

"Tom," Peggy said, "we just got notice today from Wells Fargo that Jack Burke is transferring his account over there."

"Since when? I just saw him. I went to his house with all of the documents transferring his mother's estate assets."

"The paperwork came in late Friday afternoon, around 4:30. Right after you left for the day," she said. "I didn't want to upset you over the weekend."

"Well, that's great. That SOB! I finished all the estate planning crap for his mother, and now he decides to leave. Shit." Tom stood up and slammed the office door behind him, and started pacing around the reception area. He stopped and sulked near a large potted plant by the window, but stayed within earshot.

"That's not a good sign," Lance said nodding in Tom's direction.

Peggy rolled her eyes and started typing.

Apparently in no rush to leave, Lance stayed put. He hovered behind Peggy and shifted his weight from foot to foot.

"You can leave now," Peggy said, dismissing him.

Embarrassed, Lance slinked off, muttering to himself.

Tom glared as he watched Lance walk down the hall to lick his wounds in private. Anxious to get away from Peggy and be alone himself, Tom retreated back to his office and closed the door. As he replayed his meeting with Jack Burke over and over, he paced the floor, raking his hands through his hair. He knew why Jack Burke decided to leave. Jack regretted telling him about Leon. He'd realized murder wasn't legally protected by the client-broker relationship. Burke realized he'd fucked up and now he had to leave.

When a client 'fired' Tom, he forced himself to call and ask for the reason. But in this case, Tom already knew why he'd gotten the axe. He knew too much.

Should I call Jack? Just play dumb? Not even mention Leon? Does Jack think he can't trust me? Or is he too embarrassed?

Even worse, Tom now needed to contact the bank's Compliance Office, since they'd be crawling up his ass to find out why Burke was leaving. He dreaded that call.

Seriously, though. Do I even want the Burkes as clients? Murderers? Child molesters? How will I explain this to Compliance? And what if the Burkes decide to come after me? Jack probably knows how to disguise all sorts of 'mysterious' deaths...

Tom's pulse raced and a cold sweat spread down the back of his dress shirt. He needed to calm down or he might faint. He sat down and began taking deep breaths in through his nose and blowing out through his mouth. If he flipped out and had another panic attack, they wouldn't just call an ambulance this time. Vicky might try to have him committed.

He needed another pill, but resisted. Instead, he closed his eyes, visualizing himself sitting on the shore of the riverbank, toes dangling in the cool water, peaceful and calm. Then he remembered the damn Jack Daniels bottle floating in the river. That made him anxious all over again.

He calmed down eventually and forced himself to do what he needed to do. He knocked on Lance's door, hanging wide open, as usual. Lance looked disheveled as ever, his dirty eyeglasses smeared with fingerprints and perched at the end of his nose. Lance jumped at the knock, surprised to see Tom standing in the doorway. Tom winced seeing Lance in his typical Monday attire: old stained blue khaki pants paired with bright pink socks and black plastic crocs. The neon green golf shirt, advertising a mutual fund company, completed the outfit.

Hmmm. No doubt another pilfered shirt.

The mutual fund companies gave the brokers freebies, like golf balls, hats, XXL tee shirts that fit no one, and some cheap plastic lunchboxes saying "Invest With Us" written across the top. The office kept these freebies in the lunchroom closet. They were supposed to be for clients.

"Hey, buddy! How ya' doin? Everything okay?" Lance failed to sound optimistic.

Tom ignored the greeting and barged into his partner's office. He picked up random things off Lance's desk—pictures of his three kids and wife, an autographed baseball from an Orioles game, an old cigar labeled "It's a boy!" on blue paper.

Artifacts of Lance's life intermingled with stacks of client files and generated reports, old *Wall Street Journals* stacked on the corner of the desk and a kaleidoscope that winked in the sun on the windowsill. Tom enjoyed playing with the kaleidoscope. It calmed him.

Almost as good as being stoned. I should buy one of these for myself. But then I wouldn't have anything to do when I come to talk to Lance.

He continued to turn the toy in his hands. "So, I'm sorry about losing my temper earlier. No hard feelings, right?" Tom said. "I guess I'm gonna have to call Compliance about the Burkes firing us. Yes?" Tom looked at Lance, waiting for a response.

Tom had to admit, for all of his shortcomings, Lance had mastered the corporate bullshit. All the rules, regulations and hoops their team had to jump through these days. From Compliance to Human Resources, Lance was the expert when it came to requirements from the compliance officers. The stuff drove Tom crazy, but Lance lapped it up. As far as Tom was concerned, it was the only thing Lance was good for.

"Oh, hey, yeah, no problem, man," Lance said. "Totally understandable, after all the work you just put into that account and everything." Lance smiled and shrugged his shoulders. "But, yeah, we're definitely gonna have to call Frank in Compliance, make sure there aren't any misconduct allegations. The usual garbage, you know the drill. Hey. I can call them. No problem." Lance grinned again, while Tom played with the kaleidoscope.

Aha. Drumroll please. That's what I was waiting for.

"Thanks, man. But, hey, while we're on the subject of allegations..." Tom took a deep breath and continued, "So, here's the thing. What if one of our clients, it doesn't matter which one, confesses something to us, something illegal... Where does that leave us? From a liability standpoint, I mean."

Lance stared at Tom and blinked several times. "What do you mean 'from a liability standpoint'? Because you know, liability is a slippery slope. Do you mean like, if someone did something illegal, could we go to jail, that kind of liability? Or liability like, we're under obligation to report it to the authorities, liability? Because I feel like that's a totally different thing, right? We can't control our clients. Most of them are totally whacked!"

Tom took another deep breath to calm down before he spoke. "Let's say I may or may not be privy to information that's illegal. Immoral. In fact, it's criminal. For the sake of argument, let's just say, someone flat out confesses a crime to one of us— hell, let's say they confess it to me. In that case, does that confession in any way obligate or implicate me? Am I legally bound to report it to the authorities? The SCC? Anybody?"

For a long time, Lance didn't say a word. He pushed his dirty glasses up on his greasy face again, and then ran his fingers across his unshaven face. At last, he spoke. "Buddy, are you in a roundabout, half-assed kind of way, trying to tell me one of our clients confessed to killing someone? Is that what you're saying?"

"Yes," Tom blurted. He kept playing with the kaleidoscope flipping it almost violently. "Yes, that's exactly what I'm saying."

For once in his life, Lance didn't elaborate, or pontificate. He didn't lecture or start spouting off statistics about how many financial advisors go to prison each year or how many murders occur in the metropolitan Baltimore/Washington area in any given month. He looked Tom straight in the eyes. "No," he answered. "We are not in any way liable for crimes committed by our clients—unless we are directly involved as participants."

Tom sighed and put the kaleidoscope down on the windowsill. He walked over to his partner, slapped him lightly on the back and walked out of the office.

CHAPTER FOURTEEN

Every morning, Tom spent forty-five minutes on the elliptical machine. When he turned fifty last year, he promised Vicky he'd exercise every morning before he did anything else. So he woke up early and tackled it before he had a chance to change his mind.

The workouts didn't get any easier, especially these past six months. He'd been drinking a lot and enjoying second helpings most nights at dinner. He needed to cut back on the booze and snacks. And now he'd added Valium to the mix. He realized he had to take better care of himself.

This weekend I'll spend some time out in the garden. Weeding, mowing, maybe transplant some perennials. That'll help. Working in my garden.

With his workout completed, he ate breakfast and read the local newspaper before heading in to work. Every day, he ate the same thing—a toasted English muffin with cream cheese and smoked salmon, and one cup of coffee.

In the background he heard his wife chattering about something. He grunted and nodded between bites of the English muffin, invisible under the weight of cream cheese and the salty, smoked fish.

He put on his reading glasses. The local newspaper, a pathetic and opinionated left-wing rag not worth reading, annoyed Tom and Vicky every day. Vicky, a former journalist, criticized the lack of content and the ineptitude of the writers. At least once a week, they agreed they should cancel their subscription, but it remained their chief source of local news, gossip and the obituaries. Tom found himself turning to the obits right after a quick glance at the headlines, a loosely used term for *The Town Crier*. Tom thought he'd like to cry most days after reading it.

He took a huge bite of his muffin, and chewed noisily as he skimmed the newspaper. Before he had swallowed, he screamed out, "Holy shit! Vicky! Dennis Bumpkin is dead! Died Friday!"

"What? What did you just say?"

"Fucking Dennis Bumpkin! His obituary is right here." Tom slapped the newspaper onto the table. "Son of a bitch. That cold-hearted bastard, I thought he was too mean to die. Ever."

He folded the paper in half and handed it over to Vicky.

"Yep. That's him all right. Nice picture, though."

Tom rolled his eyes. Vicky always needed to say something nice about everyone.

She continued to read, scanning and moving her finger to keep her place. "Hmm. Dennis Dunlap, 78, survived by wife, Nancy and daughter, Julie. Died unexpectedly. Huh, that's interesting."

"Well, no doubt, that prick was too cheap to pay for a hospital room," Tom said. "I'm sure he refused treatment even if he went."

"Tom, be nice. The man just died."

Tom scowled again and kept eating.

"It says he died suddenly and unexpectedly," Vicky said. "And further down, it says: 'in lieu of flowers, donations may be made to a charity of your choice.' Maybe he had a heart attack?" Vicky looked up from the newspaper for Tom's reaction.

"Yeah. I'll have to call Walter. Remember the guy I went to high school with? He's still working at the nursery. He'll have the scoop." Tom got up from the table, popped the last bite of breakfast in his mouth, and grabbed his wife's ponytail before he went upstairs to shower.

Tom decided to visit Walter in person the next day at the nursery, where he found him repotting roses.

"That son of a bitch died trimming hedges," Walter said. "By the time anyone got to him, he'd been dead for hours. But get this, man, this is classic Dennis. He was out driving around, spying on his employees, as usual. To check up on this new kid named Toby. Kind of a stoner-type. Anyway, Toby had been working out at the Stab's farm all week—you remember the place? The doctor who lives all the way in the southern part of the county?" Walter waited for him to confirm.

Tom coughed and nodded. *The Stab's? Fucking unbelievable.*

"So anyway, he drove out to Dr. Stab's. The place is in the middle of bumfuck, right? Dennis parked close to the road and walked up toward the property... I guess so the kid didn't know he was coming. A surprise attack."

I still can't believe the Stabs are part of this whole thing.

For a minute Tom got anxious again and sweat broke out on his upper lip. Thinking about that couple made him queasy. He forced himself to listen to Walter.

"So, he got closer to where the kid worked. I heard he even had his damned binoculars with him. He must've found a spot where he could see what Toby was doing. The kid was trimming arborvitae bushes. I figure Dennis didn't like what he saw. Pissed as hell, he probably charged up from behind the tree and scared the kid half to death. Told him he worked 'as slow as molasses in January.' Some things never change, right?"

Walter paused and wiped his face with a red handkerchief.

"Now, I should mention, this is Toby's version of the story. Obviously, Dennis ain't around to tell his side." Walter chuckled before he continued, "But anyway, Dennis started bitching at the kid. Told him he worked way too slow. He went ballistic. Fired the poor bastard on the spot." Walter stopped to take a noisy gulp from his water jug. "Man, I hate arborvitae. Absolute junk."

"True," Tom agreed. He abhorred arborvitae himself. Then, he realized he needed to redirect the discussion. "So, what happened? Heart attack?"

"No," Walter said. "Dennis told the kid to take the truck back to the nursery and turn in his tools. Toby got so upset, he decided to drive out to The Curve Inn. That place out on Route 15? Too embarrassed to go back to the nursery."

Again, Tom nodded.

"So, the kid hung out at the bar for the rest of the afternoon, and then left the truck there 'cause he had too much to drink. Called his girlfriend to come pick him up. Didn't return the truck until the next day. When he showed up to return his tools and the truck, the manager was confused. Didn't know Dennis had showed up at Dr. Stab's place and fired him.

"But get this. *No one* knew he got fired, and Dennis was missing. Dennis had planned to drive up to Penn State the previous afternoon, but he never made it. His wife called all over looking for him. His buddy at State College left a message on the answering machine, saying he figured Dennis changed his mind about coming up."

Walter took another swig from his water jug before he continued.

"Nancy had been out running errands all day, 'cause she thought Dennis would be out. She was gone for six or seven hours," said Walter. "The answering machine message caused her to start looking around for him. Couldn't find him anywhere. Not at home or at the nursery. Didn't answer his cell. No sign of his truck anywhere. She called their daughter and they looked for him all night. The police wouldn't do anything for twenty-four hours."

Although mesmerized by the story, Tom had trouble concentrating. Images of the Stabs kept popping into his head. *Maybe they killed him. Or kidnapped him? Or the creepy butler has him.*

Walter bent down to tie his shoe and continued. "When Toby showed up at the nursery and admitted Dennis fired him, the manager called the cops. They showed up pretty quick and drove Nancy and the daughter out to the Stab's, but nobody was home. They found Dennis' truck by the side of the service road. A couple minutes later, they found him lying beside the arborvitae, dead as a doornail, swollen, black and blue."

"God! What happened to him? Are the Stabs behind this? Did they torture him? Beat him to death?"

A puzzled look crossed Walter's face. "Bee stings," he said. "Must've come across a huge hive and they stung him to death. You remember, he was allergic as hell, always carried that Epipen with him everywhere?"

Tom nodded. Dennis never went anywhere without it.

Walter kept talking. "See, the thing is, he must've left the pen in the truck—along with his cell. Maybe decided spur of the minute to stop and spy on Toby. That son of a bitch thought to grab his binoculars, but not his phone or the Epi-pen."

Walter shook his head in disgust.

"Anyway, Toby acted all broken up about it. He told the police and Nancy that he tried to tell Dennis about the hive. That was why he had been trimming the bushes so slowly. He saw the hive and tried to avoid getting stung. But you know Dennis. Once he lost his temper, you couldn't tell him anything."

"Awful," Tom said. *I still wonder if the Stabs were behind this.*

"Yep. A real mess. Anaphylactic shock. Downright gruesome. Distorted his face, all black and blue, with his tongue sticking out. Horrible for his wife to see."

Walter looked around and made sure no one could hear them. He leaned in and whispered, "I heard the turkey vultures had to be chased off. They were already starting in on him."

"Jesus," Tom said. "Even Dennis didn't deserve to go out like that. Hey man, thanks for the info. You going to the funeral next week—Tuesday, I think the newspaper said?"

"Nah, I'm scheduled to work," Walter said. "They were lookin' for volunteers, and I was the first one to sign up. No sense pretending I liked that prick. Do you know, I heard his will stated the Country Bumpkin shouldn't close for his funeral? He was one miserly bastard."

"Seriously? No way," Tom said.

Walter bobbed his head up and down. "I know! Word on the street is, if you show up to the funeral, your pay is gonna be docked anyway—unless it was already your scheduled day off. I'll be damned if I'm gonna lose a day's pay for that SOB." Walter took off his baseball cap and wiped sweat from his forehead with the back of his sleeve.

Tom nodded in agreement. He'd never forget how Dennis had behaved when Tom's grandmother had died after a long battle with Alzheimer's. It was August following his sophomore year of college and Tom had been working the landscaping detail at the nursery all summer. Dennis pitched a fit when Tom told him he'd be missing work to go to his grandmother's funeral. In fact, he deliberately cut his hours to the bone for the rest of the summer. What a nasty prick.

When Tom did manage to get hours, it was spent trimming Christmas trees, mowing Dennis' lawn or splitting logs for Dennis' wood stove at home. In a good week, he got to repot roses at the nursery for a couple of days. He had no choice. He did whatever shitty, grunt work Dennis had in mind for him on any particular day.

The Christmas tree trimming sucked the most—although splitting wood came in as a close second. Dennis' landscapers, already underpaid, also dealt with some ridiculous restrictions. No shorts—ever. No music at all, not even the tiny transistor radio the foreman had tried to sneak onto some of the longer jobs. Workers had one ten-minute break in the morning and a half-hour (unpaid, of course) for lunch at 1:00. In the summer, employees often passed out from dehydration and heat exhaustion.

Over the years, Dennis had done some rotten things to his employees, and Tom had wondered if his boss ever knew who had unloaded to the Department of Labor about "farm workers." That problem had been solved. Now Dennis would never know.

He needed to get going, so Tom wrapped up the conversation. "Yeah, well, man, I've got to get home. I might swing by the funeral, just to check it out. Never know who might be there." Tom noticed Walter's eyebrow's raise. "Anyway, I always liked his wife. Nancy was always nice to me. I can't imagine how she's gonna run that business by herself? He controlled everything. I never could figure out why she stayed married to him all those years."

"The same reason most unhappy people stay married, chief." A smirk slid across Walter's face. "Money."

CHAPTER FIFTEEN

Tom daydreamed when he drove home after work the next day. Ever since he'd found out about Dennis, he knew he needed to confront his own mortality. He'd envisioned and sustained a successful career, starting back in the fourth grade when he brought his tiny briefcase to school. The black vinyl case had been a gift from his grandfather, a wealthy stockbroker.

"Tommy, you're going to be a rich man someday," Pops had told him.

Tom attributed his common sense and money smarts to Pops who told him stories about market crashes, depressions, recessions and blue-chip stocks.

He worked hard, even as a kid. A paper route at twelve and by fifteen landed his job at the Country Bumpkin working for Dennis. Dennis demanded a lot from his laborers, but it taught Tom about people.

In the past fifteen years he had earned a lot of money as a financial advisor, but the world of high finance chiseled away at him. Over the years, he tamed some crazy, demanding clients. But he'd lost the fire in his belly.

On a whim, he pulled a U-turn and headed into town toward the Country Bumpkin. *Something's telling me I need to go and buy some plants today.*

He filled a large cart with a mix of annuals and perennials and found a struggling maple tree in the reduced-for-quick-sale section. No sign of any of the old employees he knew. They were probably still at Dennis' wake.

A familiar voice stopped him dead in his tracks. "Well, well. Fancy meeting you here!"

Shit. Mina Stab!

Mina whirled around with her cart and cornered him beside the checkout counter.

"Mina. Hi."

"That's quite a lot of plants you're buying there, Thomas. Don't tell me you're doing the work yourself?"

"Well, yeah. I mean I enjoy puttering in the garden. I put most of our landscaping in at our house myself," Tom said.

"Really? I never pictured you for the type to get your hands dirty. Hmm..."

Is that an insult or a compliment? "Yep. I'm a landscaper from way back. As a matter of fact, I worked here as a kid. Through high school, college. Learned a lot."

"Oh, well then you heard the sad news about the owner? Terrible tragedy. And on our property! What a mess. All those police reports, the *coroner*. Dreadful ordeal. So unpleasant for us."

Mina paused and peered at Tom over her enormous black sunglasses.

"Of course we felt awful. But I didn't appreciate anyone insinuating our beehives were to blame for that man's death. Innocent beautiful creatures, and so misunderstood. As a matter of fact, I've just come from the funeral—to pay my respects. Oh, and to pay off the balance of our bill and terminate our contract. We simply can't do business with such... unprofessional people."

That explains the black mini skirt and tiger print scarf.

"Ah. You're going to stop doing business with them? Because he died working on your property?"

"Well, it's unprofessional. To die working on someone's landscaping. It's inexcusable." She glared at Tom as if he were a complete idiot. "Why would I want to continue working with people like *that*?"

"Well, I, uh. That's an interesting question, Mina. But—"

"Thomas, for God's sake," Mina interrupted. "If you died at my home, while we were reviewing our accounts, I'd have to fire you. And your firm." Mina appeared to be completely disgusted.

"But, if I were dead, no matter where I'd been working, we'd no longer be doing business together. I mean—"

"Well, obviously. But if you had the audacity to die in my home, I'd be forced to sue your estate. For personal distress."

Tom ran his hand through his hair. *Oh God. This is getting worse.* "Okay. I get the idea. Well, it's been nice chatting, but I need to get these plants home and into the ground. Tell Harry I said hello."

"Certainly, I will." Mina removed her sunglasses and surveyed Tom and his overflowing cart. "So, you'll be putting these plants in today? Tomorrow?"

"That's the plan," Tom said. "Over the weekend, at least. It's a lot to plant in one day. I'll pace myself and see how it goes."

"Hmm. I don't believe you. What's your address?"

"What? My address? Why?"

"Because I plan to drive out to see for myself, that's why."

Shock and fear overcame Tom.

"What's wrong, are you embarrassed? You don't want me to see where you live? Is it some sort of hovel? Are you ashamed? You've been to our home dozens of time, but you've never invited us to visit you and your wife, Nicky!"

"Vicky," Tom said. "My wife's name is Vicky."

Mina waved her hand in disgust. "Yes, yes. Whatever. Give me the address. I want to see your work." While she waited, Mina rooted around in her purse. She pulled out a small bag of Swedish Fish and ripped it open. She started to put one in her mouth but stopped and offered the bag to Tom.

"Candy? Oh, that's right. You don't care for my favorite candy. I'm still trying to get over not being able to become a stockholder. I can't bring myself to believe they're made by Cadbury in Canada. I think you lied to me." She grabbed a few fish and ate them one at a time while she waited.

Tom stood motionless for a minute, trying to decide what to do. *Jesus. She wants my address? I'm fucked. I have to give it to her, I guess.*

"Well? I don't have all day." Mina took out her cell phone. "Give it to me and I'll put it in my GPS. I'll stop out this weekend."

Stunned, Tom mumbled the address and waved goodbye as she walked up to the Customer Service counter.

"Goodbye, Thomas. I'll see you soon."

Tom watched as Mina pulled out her checkbook and terrorized the young clerk at the counter. He made his way to the checkout at the far end of the store and raced to put the plants in the trunk of his car.

When he drove through his gated community's entrance, his spirits lifted a bit. The sight of his beautiful neighborhood, bordered by the manicured lawns and the back nine of the CCC—the esteemed Cray Country Club—golf course raised his spirits.

But, fucking Mina. Seriously. Was she going to show up here? And want to meet Vicky? Oh, God. Why does she keep pulling this shit? I need a drink.

He pulled into his driveway, and saw he needed to cut the grass and trim some of the shrubs. Plus he needed to divide and transplant the perennial plants in the front yard before the end of the summer. He'd not kept up with his yard work. And now he had all those new plants to put in. He hoped it would help him relax. He decided to hold off on having a beer until after he'd finished as a reward for himself.

He walked into the house and called for Vicky, but no one answered. She must have gone out with the girls. They sure liked to spend his money. Not that he begrudged them anything, but he disliked being taken advantage of. His family had no clue how hard he worked for the money they churned into the economy.

He changed clothes and headed out to get started. The late afternoon sun perked him up while he organized the new plants. He started to dig holes for them, when he spotted a family of swallows flying around his bluebird box. The blasted things had built another nest there again.

All summer he ripped out their nests. The swallows, notorious squatters, invaded the bluebird boxes and his mailbox. He liked the bluebirds, and he appreciated their tidy nests, but the swallow's nests looked dirty and messy. This irritated him, but he decided to deal with them after he finished the other planting and mowing.

Don't let this upset you. It's not worth it. Get the stuff planted. Worry about the birds later.

After about an hour and a half, he had everything planted but the tree. So he decided to start mowing to give his knees and back a rest.

He climbed on the John Deere, and tooled around his lawn, turning and maneuvering around his many gardens and shrubs. Vicky claimed to enjoy mowing, but Tom figured it was just so she could work on her tan.

Over the years, his landscaping exploded all over the property. Beautiful mature trees, evergreens, shrubs and multitudes of native plants popped from every corner of the yard.

Damn it. I'm good at this shit. Look at this! Started from nothing. Now something always blooms, from early spring through the fall. And in the winter I've got the evergreens. This is why I do this! I think my blood pressure dropped twenty points.

As he mowed, one of the squatter swallows flew across the yard and dove perilously close to Tom's head. *What the hell? Thank God I'm wearing a hat!*

In fact Tom always wore a hat when working outdoors. Not only did it protect him from the sun, it also put another layer between him and nature. As a little kid, he'd watched as his favorite uncle suffered a bird attack. A bird had swooped in from a copse of trees and snatched the toupee right off his head. The bird flapped away to its nest in an enormous white pine tree carrying the furry prize in its beak.

The family got a glimpse of the "real" Uncle John, sans his toupee. The bird's sharp claws and beak had lacerated his scalp and he ended up in the emergency room. Tom had recurring nightmares about that attack for years.

He kept mowing, glancing around the yard, looking for the dive-bombing bird. He started sweating and felt his heart beating very fast. He knew it was silly for a grown man to be afraid of birds, but he couldn't help it.

Sure enough, after a few minutes, the bird came back, flying beside him at almost eye level, and then circled around him as he bumped across the lawn. Quickly it sped off, flying up and away from the mower, only to return at full speed, aimed for his head. Tom turned off the mower and ran into the garage cursing, "Fucking bird. God damn it! This is crazy."

He looked around to make sure it hadn't followed him. He peered out from the open garage door, looking not only for the predator bird, but to see if the neighbors might have witnessed any of this unfold. He didn't see anyone outside, but spotted the bird flying in circles around the yard, and then flying to the bluebird box at the back of the property.

"Just wait, asshole," Tom said to the bird, as he watched it flying around. "That box isn't for *you*, it's a blue bird box. Stupid fucking thing." He looked around again to make sure no one had heard him talking to himself.

Damn it. I can't let a stupid bird stop me from mowing the grass. What can I do?

He looked around the garage for something to defend himself. And then, he saw the perfect weapon against this flying menace, perched innocently on its rightful hook.

Tom reached over, unzipped the protective cover, grabbed the tennis racket and climbed back on the lawn tractor. Sure enough, as if on cue, the bird approached again, but Tom was ready for it.

He swung at the bird, missing it completely, but kept mowing. He rode up and down the lawn, circling the roses and along the border row of cryptomeria. He waved the tennis racket and took an occasional swing in mid-air just in case it returned.

He cut the final swaths of grass and took one last swipe at the absent bird before heading back into his garage. He parked the mower in the corner, ready to go into the house. Then he saw her.

Oh, shit. Oh, no. No.

Mina Stab stood transfixed at the end of his driveway, leaning on her car.

"Mina?" he whimpered.

For a moment she did nothing. Then she fumbled with her keys and climbed in the car.

Tom ran over to her, wondering what he could say. "Mina, stop! I can explain."

She rolled down her window a few inches and glared at Tom.

"Mina, I know this looks a little strange, but..."

"What in God's name were you doing, Thomas?"

"Well, see, there was this bird, and it was attacking me..."

Mina put up her hand to stop him. "Thomas, this is very disturbing. I stopped by to see your landscaping. I never expected to see you conducting yourself in such a manner. And now, to see you attacking innocent birds in your backyard? With a tennis racket? How could you? How cruel. Frankly, I'm shocked. Goodbye, Thomas."

"Mina, wait. I can explain."

But she rolled up her window and fastened her seat belt. She started to pull out of the driveway but instead stopped and rolled down the window. She motioned Tom over to the car.

Good. She's gonna let me explain.

"Oh, Thomas, I almost forgot to tell you. Your guard at the gate gave me a terrible time. He wanted to see my driver's license. Can you imagine? The nerve! I told him who I was. He should've recognized my name and waved me in. He should be fired."

She backed out and pulled away before Tom could respond.

***

Tom sat down at the kitchen table and started in on the Heineken. Before he knew it, he'd downed four beers. He heard the garage door opening, but didn't move. When his family burst in lugging grocery bags to the center island, he barely looked up. Vicky and the girls walked over to the kitchen table, but he didn't greet them.

"Dad, you look... weird," Jane said. "And you're all sweaty. Gross."

"Yeah, gross, Dad," Sophie said as she wrinkled her nose in disgust. "You smell, too."

"I've been doing yard work!" Tom yelled. "What's wrong with you people? Haven't you ever seen anyone doing yard work before? Mowing grass? Pulling weeds? Sorry to embarrass you with my blue-collar hobbies." He stomped to the fridge for another beer.

"Hon, are you okay? Is something wrong?" Vicky asked as she reached for his face. "You look stressed... flushed, or something."

"I'm fine, damn it. Just fine. First, the stupid birds attack me, then Mina showed up here to spy on me and look at the new plants I just bought at the Country Bumpkin. I didn't know she'd pulled into the driveway. She saw me on the riding mower, swatting at the birds with my tennis racket. And now the three of you are crawling up my ass because I'm a little dirty and sweaty. Jesus H. Christ." Tom stopped ranting when Vicky whirled around.

"What is wrong with you? Raving like a lunatic, talking about birds attacking you and tennis rackets and Mina Stab spying on you? You're acting crazy."

"Yeah," Sophie said. "Crazy!"

"That's enough, you," Vicky said. She pointed a finger at her youngest child and then redirected her attention to Tom. "Mommy needs to talk to Daddy. Girls, can you put the groceries away for me, please?"

"Who's Mommy?" Jane said. "I haven't called you Mommy in like fifteen years. Maybe more."

"Thanks for reminding me, dear," Vicky said. "Just do it."

The girls both stifled giggles and unloaded the groceries. Vicky grabbed Tom's hand and led him out of the kitchen and into the family room to talk in private.

She reached up and touched his face. Worry creased her brow. "Tom, what in God's name is going on with you? Did you take your medicine today? I think I should call the doctor." Vicky searched her phone for the doctor's number. "I wonder if he has any office hours left today."

"Stop. Vicky, I mean it. Stop. No doctor. I'm okay." He tried to steady his shaking voice. He looked at her and took a few deep breaths before he continued. "I'm okay. It's been a very strange week. Finding out Dennis died, talking to Walt, all the crap going on with my clients."

He ran his fingers through his hair.

"The damn swallows are back in the bluebird box, dive-bombing me. I ran into Mina at the Country Bumpkin and she demanded my address so she could check out our landscaping. Oh, and meet *you*."

He stopped and smiled at Vicky.

"Then she saw me swatting the tennis racket. I was so angry at that stupid bird. I'm tired, but I'm okay, honest. Embarrassed mostly." He reached out and grabbed her into a big squeeze.

Vicky smiled at him before she pulled away. "Ugh, Honey, you *are* sweaty. No offense. Go take a shower." She smiled and patted his cheek again. "Seriously, Tom. Go take a long, hot shower. You'll feel better."

She walked back to the kitchen where the girls pretended to put away the groceries. He heard her talking to them in hushed tones he couldn't make out. Embarrassed and out of sorts, he walked upstairs to take a shower, and clear his head.

He closed the bathroom door and went straight to the medicine cabinet. He rifled through the shelves until he found what he wanted... what he needed—the tiny plastic bottle to calm his frazzled nerves. He shook out a pill, dry swallowed it, and then sat on the closed toilet seat with his head in his hands.

When the Valium kicked in, his pulse slowed, his heart stopped racing, and his breathing returned to normal again. These damn panic attacks were coming more often now. It used to happen maybe a couple of times a year max, and he talked himself out of it. Deep breaths and a shot of Scotch had been enough. Now three or four times a week the panic attacks crippled him.

At work one day last month, he'd convinced himself he was having a heart attack. A visit to his doctor of twenty years confirmed severe anxiety, not a heart attack. He'd been scolded for gaining twenty pounds and not taking his blood pressure meds. "Tom, get some exercise and take a vacation. You need to relax."

He'd prescribed a low dose of Valium to take the edge off, but only when Tom felt an attack coming on. "Not to be used daily," the prescription label said, and Tom listened to that advice; after all, his doctor wanted to spare him drug addiction in addition to his other bad habits. He'd promised to take the pills only when the anxiety got extreme, like today.

And every day this week when he'd needed them.

When he calmed down, he saw how irrationally he had behaved. But at the time, it had made perfect sense to drive around on his lawn mower with a tennis racket, swatting at birds. The bird hadn't actually attacked him, but he'd seen it happen when he was a kid. When that deranged bird mauled

Uncle John and stole his toupee. No wonder shrinks said childhood traumas led to seriously fucked-up adults.

I know the family doctor thinks I need therapy, but Jesus, who has time for therapy? Oh sure, it sounds great in theory, going in to spill your guts to some hotshot PhD who wants to charge big bucks and judge you by your crazy childhood or your relationship with your mother.

He stepped into the hot, steamy shower and closed his eyes tight.

I can't keep this up. I'll have a heart attack, or Vicky will have me committed—if she doesn't divorce me first.

He stood under the scalding shower and had what he could only describe as a true epiphany. Peace washed over him in soapy waves as he lathered and scrubbed.

Of course. It all makes perfect sense now. Why didn't I think of it before?

He smiled and breathed a sigh of relief. He knew exactly what he needed to do.

CHAPTER SIXTEEN

By 7:30 most mornings, Tom had finished his workout on the elliptical, showered, shaved and eaten breakfast. Today, he groaned, rolled out of bed, and faced the red-eyed bloated man staring back at him in the mirror. Sleep deprived, he pondered whether a stiff Bloody Mary might help more than a cup of coffee.

He thought a Swedish massage might help him relax, so he called to schedule one for tomorrow afternoon. But the thought of anything Swedish reminded him of Mina, so immediately he rescheduled for a deep tissue instead, and refilled his Valium prescription. *Just till I get through this ordeal.*

Instead of going to the office, he wished he could stay home to binge-watch "Breaking Bad" and eat Swedish Fish in front of the TV. Damn that Mina Stab. Ever since their appointment, he'd craved those blasted things, broken tooth and all. But he needed to get through today. No matter how much sleep he'd lost these past few months, or how much he agonized over the details, he knew he'd made the right decision about his future.

After he showered and grabbed some coffee he felt well enough to go to the office. Once there, he wrapped up the routine tasks and crunched the numbers for the umpteenth time to ensure his plan would work. Then, he called Jim Doyle and invited him to lunch at the Cray Country Club. Doyle, too cheap to spring for a membership himself, enjoyed mooching off Tom. So, while Peggy played with her phone, and Lance badgered a client in his office, Tom sneaked out without a word.

He planned to text Peggy when he got to the club and claim he'd forgotten about his meeting with Doyle.

Although outdated since its heyday in the 1960s, the club remained a decent place to go for a private lunch meeting. A buxom hostess dressed in a tight polyester pantsuit seated them quickly and sent the mousy server over to take their drink orders. Tom and Doyle shared political banter and small talk for a few minutes when Tom sprung his plan. He gave a few details then asked Doyle what he thought.

"Okay, let me get this straight," Doyle said. "You're leaving Global Quest International? You're going to throw away your career—the thing you have spent your entire adult life building, hell most of your childhood too, for that matter—on a fucking hobby? Man, have you lost your mind! What about Vicky and the girls? How are you gonna pay for college? How are you gonna pay your mortgage? Hell, for that matter, how are you gonna pay for my lunch today?" Doyle glared at Tom and took a long swig of Jameson from his highball.

"Look," said Tom taking a gulp from his water glass, "I know it sounds crazy, but I've run the numbers, Doyle. I can make it work. This life is killing me. My gums are bleeding, and my bowels are blowing up from the daily diarrhea. Every day I see bigger fistfuls of my hair in the shower drain. I need to jump off this merry-go-round while I can." He looked into Doyle's eyes. "I have to do this, Jim."

Doyle looked up from his drink and sighed. "Buddy. As long as I've known you, I've never managed to talk you out of anything. Why in the hell should I try now?" He smiled and shook his head. "I mean, man, I don't know what's going on with you. You've got it made! A beautiful house, a beautiful wife, great kids, primo job, membership at the CCC, 'the Benz'... how can you throw all this away on some fly-by-night idea? What is this, a midlife crisis?"

"I'm dead serious about this. Vicky will support me. She's been worried sick. I can't live like this anymore." Tom reached into his pocket, pulled out a handkerchief and wiped his forehead.

"Okay, brother," Doyle said. "It's your life, you gotta do what you think is right." Doyle smiled and waved the waitress over. When the young woman arrived, he leaned in close and placed a hand on her shapely rear. "Sweetheart, just keep these drinks coming. And bring my friend a double, will you? We're gonna be here for a while."

After the long lunch, which melded into an early happy hour, Tom headed back into the office. He figured by five o'clock most of the brokers and staff should be gone for the day, and he'd clean off his desk and be home by 6:30.

He never drank this early in the afternoon, and he shouldn't have driven anywhere. But it was a short drive from the club, and the Benz practically operated on autopilot.

He wobbled a bit walking into the elevator from the garage, but he made it. As he walked to his office, he heard a loud muffled argument in the distance. He recognized Peggy's shrill voice and Lance's booming bass echoing through the office corridor. Tom ambled into the reception area and came face to face with them in the throws of a shouting match.

"Why is this such a problem for you, Peggy? Do I need to read your job description to you again? How many new client business accounts have you opened in your career? Do I need to send you back to training? It's pretty simple. Look at the protocol outlined in my instructions on page seventy-eight of the procedural model and follow the formula. When I was a client administrator like you, I could bang out one of these in twenty minutes or less, I mean—"

Peggy threw the manual into the trashcan. "Lance!" she screamed. "What in the name of God makes you think anything about this process is simple? I have to log into the system, input all the data from there into the new client access database, and then transfer the account balances to the new system, not to mention, all the red tape from Compliance. Simple, my ass!"

Peggy stopped yelling to blow a strand of frizzy hair out of her face.

"You are such a pompous ass, Lance. Your manual is a worthless piece of shit. I'm sick of you boring everyone to death with your so-called interesting facts." Peggy made air quotes with her fingers. "You bore people to death—your clients, your coworkers, probably even your dog. God. Shut up. Do the work yourself if you're so good at it."

Peggy's cell phone rang in her pocket and broke the spell. She answered it and walked away from reception, passing Tom as he popped out of his office.

"What in the hell is going on?" Tom's voice sounded far away inside his head. "I could hear you two as soon as I got off the elevator."

Peggy took the phone from her ear and covered the mouthpiece with her hand, "I can't take him anymore, Tom. He's crazy. He's such a bullshitter—always the expert on everything. I'm going home. I'll text you later." She slammed the door on her way out.

Amused, Tom couldn't agree more. Even better, with his new escape plan in full swing, he could seize the opportunity to bait Lance and get more information. This sobered him up a bit. He hated them both and thought they deserved each other. Peggy was the laziest assistant known to man, and Lance was the biggest blowhard on the planet. It delighted him to see them fighting.

Tom put on his game face and prepared to play devil's advocate. He noted Lance's clothes looked more appropriate for cleaning out a garage than meeting with clients. Tom swallowed his disgust when he noticed a chunk of crusty yellow material in Lance's beard. *Gross. It must be egg from his breakfast. And what is he wearing? It's a wonder they don't fire him for a violation of the dress code.* In his untucked wrinkled shirt, baggy pleated pants and tattered loafers, he resembled a lopsided clown. Lance looked up at him through smudged eyeglasses.

Tom looked for the kaleidoscope as soon as he walked into Lance's office. He picked up the toy and immediately it calmed his nerves. "So, looks like I interrupted something pretty intense here?"

Lanced jumped at the chance to share his side of the story. "Yeah, well you know Peggy. Never can predict what kind of mood she's going to be in. Or what's gonna set her off. Right?" Lance squinted and pushed his glasses up higher on his nose. "I mean, you never know when she'll freak out and go ballistic!" Lance leaned closer to Tom and sniffed. "Hey, what? Did you have a couple of drinks at lunch, man? You reek."

"Huh, oh yeah... lunch with my buddy, Doyle. There's no stopping that crazy bastard once he starts drinking Jameson." Tom decided to play along and goad Lance for more information. "But, Jesus, how about Peggy? She gets pissed off if you ask her to do anything. And it doesn't matter whether it's in her job description or not."

Tom reached into his pocket and brought out his bag of Swedish Fish. He offered it to Lance who waved his hand to decline.

"And her damn phone is practically growing out of her hand. Always typing on it, talking to her husband or one of her kids. It's become a real problem. And that stupid little stand she has for it on her desk. What is that, I mean, like an easel or something? Where does she find these phone accessories?"

"Yeah. Agreed," Lance said, not taking the bait. "Well, I'm getting out of here. I'm already late for my basketball game with the guys."

This annoyed Tom, because "the guys" were the poor schleps Lance attached himself to several times a week at the YMCA. They had all played in high school together years ago, and continued to pretend they were good enough to run up and down a basketball court. Lance, the outsider, was frequently delegated to "referee." He even bought a red plastic whistle to wear around his neck.

Tom kept playing with the kaleidoscope, and realized Lance was acting like he wanted him to leave.

"I didn't mean to hold you up, but I wanted to let you know I need to be out tomorrow. Got some personal stuff to take care of. Are you gonna be around?" Tom smiled at his partner and waited for a response.

"Yeah. Oh, yeah, sure. I'll be here. Did you need something?"

Tom saw Lance embracing this false sense of camaraderie. "Well, I hate to ask you this, but I just realized the Stabs are coming in around ten tomorrow morning. Peggy sent a text earlier saying they called and asked if they could stop in. Nothing urgent, just some questions about their statement."

Yeah, right. Nothing urgent. Probably firing me after she saw me swatting at the birds on my lawnmower.

Tom smiled and continued, "I'd appreciate it if you could pinch-hit for me. If I break my plans with Vicky tomorrow, I'll never hear the end of it."

Lance agreed, completely unaware Tom planned to sever all ties. Tom replaced the kaleidoscope and shook his soon-to-be-ex-partner's hand.

"Thanks, Lance. You have no idea how helpful this is."

He walked out of the office whistling. The wheels were in motion.

CHAPTER SEVENTEEN

Tom woke early the next morning and drove to his favorite diner, The Blue Bomb. He took his time eating a big breakfast and sent out a couple of emails from his iPad, including a brief note to Mina explaining Lance would fill in for him today. When he checked his watch, he saw he still had plenty of time before his nine o'clock meeting at the bank with Frank Sajak, VP of Small Business Lending.

After the meeting with Doyle yesterday, he'd called Sajak, a guy he had known for years. They weren't close friends, but they had an affable business relationship. Frank agreed right away to meet with Tom, eager to hear his proposal.

A former wrestler with a wispy blond comb-over, Frank bustled across the lobby to shake hands. "Tom. Good to see you. Been a while. Since the business expo back in the spring? Come on. Let's go into my office where we can talk. Coffee?"

"No, thanks. I've had plenty already. Enough to fly up to your office." Tom tried to ignore the beads of sweat trickling down the inside of his tee shirt and the quick thumping of his heart. He concentrated on taking deep breaths, and tried to stay focused. They walked while Frank talked about his family.

Tom remembered Frank had married Tina, a total bitch, right after college. She shopped, played tennis and bullied their children non-stop. Vicky couldn't stand her, and Vicky liked everyone. Frank summarized what his kids were up to, in particular his sons, Alex and Tony. Then Tom remembered they'd lettered in a couple of sports in high school. A very athletic family.

God. Try to focus on what the man is saying.

Then something Frank said caught his attention.

"So, yeah, this lawsuit has been a real pain—hard on the kids and even harder on Tina. She's so embarrassed."

Tom stopped walking and turned to face Frank. "What? I'm sorry. Did you say lawsuit?"

"Yeah, it started out that way. As a lawsuit, I mean. But then there were complications with this awful woman attorney. Medical malpractice—Marcia Markel—ever heard of her?"

Oh, great. Marcia. This is unbelievable.

"Um, I have, I think. Does she advertise a lot? On TV?"

"Yeah. That's her. She's a total fraud." Frank lowered his voice. "You know, she has a thing for younger men. She was after my boys. That's what started this whole mess. Well, I mean, after the wrestling coach molested Alex."

Jesus H. Christ.

Tom blinked and then started to fiddle with his tie when they began walking again. "Is that right? That's awful."

"Yeah, it's been a nightmare. That woman deserves to have the book thrown at her. Well, her and that wrestling coach, Leon Burke. He should be in jail. I should've never agreed to settle out of court with the school." Frank made a grand gesture toward his office door and called to his assistant, a tiny dark-haired waif, "Hey, hold my calls."

Deep breaths, calming breaths. Hari Krishna, Krishna, Krishna, Namaste, blah, blah, blah. God, don't let me blow this. I wish I'd paid more attention to all those new-age whack jobs when they tried to explain Transcendental Meditation back in college.

Frank cracked his knuckles and put his hands on top of his desk. "Hey, enough about me. Let's talk some business. Tell me about your idea."

Tom took a deep breath and sprung his idea on Frank, happy to change the subject.

About an hour later, the two emerged from the office all smiles. Tom continued to breathe deeply, surprised it had helped him stay calm.

Frank gave his assistant some directions, then said, "Tom, I'll be back in a minute. Just need to make a few quick calls and we'll be all set."

Thirty minutes later, Frank walked over and handed him an envelope.

"Here you go, Tom. All the documents you'll need and the check. And good luck. I'll be waiting to hear from you to see how everything goes. Stick to the plan we discussed and you should be good to go. Let me know if you need anything else."

Tom accepted the envelope and tried not to cringe when Frank slapped him on the back. He made a quick exit from the bank building and jumped into his car to drive home.

Fifteen or so minutes later, he walked in to find Vicky engrossed in a Zumba fitness DVD. She waved a perplexed hello, and sauntered over to the remote control to pause her workout. After grabbing a water bottle from the coffee table she walked into the kitchen where Tom stood grinning.

"What are you doing home at eleven o'clock in the morning? Is everything all right? Are you sick? Did you get fired? *Oh, God.* You have the strangest look on your face. Should I call the doctor again?"

She rushed to grab her phone, but Tom reached out and pulled her close to him. "No, I'm fine. In fact, I'm great. I'm here to see you, to take you with me. Go change clothes. We're going out."

"What do you mean, we're going out? Where are we going? I'm not finished with my workout yet." Vicky looked annoyed. "Tom, what's going on?"

"Just play along with me, babe. Throw on some clean clothes, and come with me. It's a surprise." Confused, she stared at Tom, who grinned from ear to ear. No doubt he looked happier than she'd seen in a long time.

Vicky ran upstairs to change clothes.

"Put on something nice," Tom yelled up. "We're going out for lunch afterwards."

The sound of running water upstairs meant Vicky had decided to take a quick shower. Ten minutes later they were back in the Mercedes, driving. Tom, ready to burst with excitement, kept glancing at his pretty wife. He grabbed her hand as he drove and kissed her palm.

"Eyes on the road, cowboy," Vicky said. "We won't be having any fun if we end up in the emergency room."

Tom laughed, but released her hand as they drove through town beyond the city limits.

"Where are we going?" Vicky asked. "There's nothing out here. Nothing except... oh God. Where are we going, Tom? Tell me!"

Tom smiled and pushed buttons on the dash to access his cell phone. "Siri, call Nancy B."

"Calling Nancy B," Siri said in her electronic monotone.

Tom switched off the speaker and spoke privately. "Hi, it's me. We're here. Pulling in right now. Yes, okay. See you in a minute. Yes, she's with me. Okay. Bye."

He slowed the car as they approached the gravel parking lot, and drove up to the front door. Leaving the engine running, he beeped the horn in quick succession. A few curious customers milling around the end-of-season bargain display turned to stare. A few of them waved, and Tom waved back.

A familiar face appeared at the door and Vicky gasped. Nancy Bumpkin—widow of Dennis, and now the sole proprietor of the Country Bumpkin—wiped her hand on a rag sticking out of her overalls and smiled a sad smile. She walked to the driver's side of the car and Tom jumped out to greet her with a hug. Then he raced around to the passenger side of the Mercedes and opened the door. Looking back at Nancy, he raised a finger to the air, begging momentary pause. Nancy nodded and turned away.

"Tom?" Vicky said under her breath. "Why are we at the Country Bumpkin? To buy plants? Is this some kind of joke?"

Tom was grinning like the Cheshire cat. "Nope, no joke. In fact, I've never been more serious in my life. Come on, get out of the car for a minute." Tom put his arm around Vicky's shoulders and spun her around to face him. "I've got some big news for you, babe. We're here to buy something all right, but not a plant. Well, technically, I guess we are. Lots of them!" He pulled Vicky by the hand and walked toward Nancy.

Reaching into his pocket he pulled out the envelope he'd picked up at the bank. He opened it and pulled back the corner to peek inside.

Vicky grabbed the edge of the envelope to get a good look. A grin spread across her face as she realized his plan. "Are you saying what I think you're saying? This check... it's for... really? You really want to do this? Are you sure?"

Tom grabbed her hands, kissed her on the cheek and nodded as he looked into her eyes, waiting for her approval. "Only if you'll do it with me. I can't do it without you, Vick."

"Well, okay, then. Let's do it!"

Tom took the envelope back from Vicky, and handed it to Nancy. Nancy pulled out the contents, scanned it quickly and looked pleased.

"Well, look at that," she said. "A certified check made payable to me, Nancy Bumpkin, in the amount of $500,000. Congratulations, Tom," she said smiling. "You've just bought yourself a landscaping business. Now let's go inside and sign the paperwork."

The End

ABOUT THE AUTHOR

A graduate of The Pennsylvania State University with a Bachelor's Degree in Communications, Arts and Sciences and a Minor in English, Sandy Bush has a background in Federal, State and County Government.

In 2014 she decided to pursue freelance writing opportunities. She has published articles in the Pennsylvania School Board Association's magazine *The Bulletin*, and the online magazine *Keystone Edge* as well as work in advertising, and museum script writing for the Oil Heritage Museum, Titusville, PA.

Currently Sandy is the Area 5 Representative for Pennwriters, an organization dedicated to assisting writers of all levels and genres.

Sandy lives with her husband Todd in Pennsylvania. They are the parents of daughters Chelsea and Monica and pet parents to cats Gracie and Boo.